"How do I know you won't ask me to do something…something dangerous?" she managed.

"You don't," Dane said, playing devil's advocate as the adrenaline rush powered through his veins. "You're just gonna have to trust me," he added.

Jamilla had insisted on coming along for this ride, so she had to live with the consequences.

"For once, you're just gonna have to relax and enjoy the ride," he said. "You think you can manage that?"

He watched her debate the question, then figure out she didn't have much of a choice. It was his way or the highway and she was way too dedicated to her job to risk leaving him to his own devices. But then he saw excitement flicker in her eyes and his pulse jumped.

Sweet.

A part of her *wanted* to take a walk on the wild side with him. Even if she would never admit it to herself.

When she nodded, he revved the bike's engine. He finally had Jamilla Roussel where he wanted her. Time to stop letting her push his buttons and start pushing every one of hers.

USA TODAY bestselling author **Heidi Rice** lives in London, England. She is married with two teenage sons—which gives her rather too much of an insight into the male psyche—and also works as a film journalist. She adores her job, which involves getting swept up in a world of high emotions; sensual excitement; funny, feisty women; sexy, tortured men; and glamorous locations where laundry doesn't exist. Once she turns off her computer, she often does chores—usually involving laundry!

Books by Heidi Rice

Harlequin Presents

A Forbidden Night with the Housekeeper
Innocent's Desert Wedding Contract

Hot Summer Nights with a Billionaire

One Wild Night with her Enemy

Passion in Paradise

My Shocking Monte Carlo Confession

The Christmas Princess Swap

The Royal Pregnancy Test

Secrets of Billionaire Siblings

The Billionaire's Proposition in Paris
The CEO's Impossible Heir

Visit the Author Profile page
at Harlequin.com for more titles.

Heidi Rice

BANISHED PRINCE TO DESERT BOSS

Recycling programs
for this product may
not exist in your area.

ISBN-13: 978-1-335-56959-2

Banished Prince to Desert Boss

Copyright © 2022 by Heidi Rice

For questions and comments about the quality of this book,
please contact us at CustomerService@Harlequin.com.

Harlequin Enterprises ULC
22 Adelaide St. West, 41st Floor
Toronto, Ontario M5H 4E3, Canada
www.Harlequin.com

Printed in U.S.A.

BANISHED PRINCE TO
DESERT BOSS

This book is dedicated to my mum, who reads my books and tells me she loves them, even though there's no golf or bowls in them (and there never will be).

CHAPTER ONE

A COMBINATION OF nerves, heat exhaustion and tightly leashed fury tied Jamilla Omar Roussel's stomach into knots as she watched the Zafari royal jet, its red and gold insignia glinting in the sunshine, land on the desert airstrip.

She glanced surreptitiously at her watch for about the ten thousandth time that afternoon.

You're an hour late, you—

She cut off the name she wanted to call Dane Jones—the jet's illustrious passenger, and the man she was here to greet officially on behalf of her employer, Sheikh Karim Jamal Amari Khan—before it could properly register, let alone spill out of her mouth.

She would not stoop to the same level as the Manhattan playboy being flown in to replace her employer by calling him names.

Jones was Karim Khan's half-brother, the result of King Abdullah's rocky marriage to his fourth wife, American socialite Kitty Jones. And even if Jones didn't use his father's surname or his royal title and had never even visited his homeland since his parents' divorce at the age of five, he was the only person Zafar's rather traditional ruling council would accept to represent the country in Karim's absence. The important trade mission to Europe had been in the offing for two years and was due to start next week, but Karim and Orla had decided to remain in their home in Ireland with their three-year-old son Hasan to await the birth of their twins when Orla had been diagnosed with gestational hypertension two days ago. Karim had refused point-blank to leave his family to embark on the tour alone and as many of the dates and events could not be rearranged at such short notice, calling on his half-brother to step in had been the only way to avoid cancelling the tour altogether.

Anxious concern for her friend Orla tightened the knots in Jamilla's stomach…

You can do this, Milla. You have to.

At the age of only twenty-four she had just become the Zafari royal family's chief diplomatic aide. She spoke six languages fluently—plus the four local dialects. She had a master's degree in political science from the neighbouring University of Narabia and in the last few years had worked her way up from being the Queen's personal assistant at the palace to Karim and Orla's right-hand woman in affairs of the Zafari state… Orla's pregnancy scare had handed Jamilla a sudden promotion which she would never have expected, or wanted in these circumstances, but which was still an opportunity to consolidate her position in the royal court. And finally offer her a chance to travel to countries outside the kingdom.

An exciting, challenging opportunity she absolutely refused to fail at.

And not just because it would give her career an impressive boost if she could pull this off—and turn a Manhattan playboy into a royal prince—but because Karim and Orla and Zafar were counting on her.

She dabbed her brow with her now sodden tissue while blinking furiously to keep the sweat—which had gone from a trickle to a flood ten minutes ago—out of her eyes. As the luxury jet taxied to a stop, she reviewed the detailed itinerary for the coming week of preparations in Zafar, which she had finalised late last night and had planned to brief the stand-in head of state on during the two-hour drive back to the Palace of the Kings. A cloud rose from the runway, covering her and the delegation of officials standing next to her to greet their new temporary head of state too in a spray of fine grit.

Their exceptionally *late* new temporary head of state.

Jamilla gritted her teeth against the wave of

misery, and pressed sweaty palms to the tailored knee-length grey pencil skirt she'd donned that morning, but which now felt like a damp strait-jacket. She'd opted for a modern professional look over traditional garb. Unfortunately, when choosing not to wear the full, flowing dark desert robes intended to maintain a woman's modesty as much as regulate her body heat, Jamilla hadn't factored in the practical aspects of wearing a fitted designer suit and four-inch heels for any length of time in the afternoon sun.

She straightened her spine, swallowed down the increasingly persistent nausea and ignored the low-grade headache gripping her skull. Once she had greeted the American billionaire and introduced him to the long line of dignitaries, she would forego the briefing and take the opportunity to relax in the front seat of the air-conditioned limo while they travelled back to the Palace.

She was far too frazzled now to think clearly—and she probably looked an absolute state, not at all the first impression she had intended to make. While she had planned to hit the ground running today—as they had only eight days before flying to Europe to begin their royal tour—it would make more sense to ease Jones in slowly. Tomorrow would be soon enough to arrange their first proper briefing—and give

Jamilla the chance to set the right tone for their future working relationship.

She lifted an arm, heavy with fatigue, to shield her eyes from the brutal sunshine as the ground crew wheeled the jet's metal stairs into place and the door opened.

The elderly ruling council member who had travelled to New York to accompany Dane Jones back to the kingdom on Karim's orders appeared first, followed by his staff, the cabin crew, the pilot and the co-pilot. As they all exited the aircraft, then either climbed into cars to head back to the Palace or joined the welcoming committee, the jet's door remained open for two… Three… Curse it, four more minutes.

What is he waiting for? An even bigger entrance? Hasn't he delayed us all enough already?

Jamilla was ready to weep, the sweat stains on her suit now probably visible from space, when a tall, broad figure appeared in the plane's doorway.

Finally.

He made his way down the aircraft stairs.

She blinked, wiped her brow again, her heart jumping into her throat as something warm and solid wedged itself between her damp thighs.

Goodness.

She pushed a breath out, drew in another.

She'd seen photos of Dane Jones in the celebrity magazines and websites she checked each month—purely for professional purposes. She needed to know who was who in the VIP world, as the Khans enjoyed hosting events in the kingdom. Although Karim's half-brother had never accepted any of the invitations Jamilla had extended to him, she knew he was an exceptionally handsome man. Not really surprising, given that he was Karim's blood relation.

But as he stepped onto the desert floor, a leather bag slung over his shoulder, her gaze absorbed every breathtaking detail. The fluid, almost predatory gait, the worn jeans hanging loosely on narrow hips, the black T-shirt moulded to defined pecs, the chiselled cheekbones, the heavy stubble covering a hard jaw and the wavy hair—a burnished bronze streaked with sun-bleached gold—long enough to curl around his ears, topped by a baseball cap with a New York Yankees logo.

She swallowed past the lump of something raw and unfamiliar in her throat.

Okay.

She sucked in another crucial breath, beginning to feel light-headed—which had to be the heat, surely. As Dane Jones strode towards her, he lifted his head to reveal dark aviator sunglasses. His head dipped, his gaze cruising the length of her body, and no doubt taking in the sodden power suit. She felt the searing perusal everywhere as the temperature shot up another few thousand degrees.

'Hey,' he said, his voice a husky rasp, as if he'd just woken up. Maybe he had.

They'd been informed the delegation from Zafar had been forced to wake him up at his penthouse apartment when he hadn't shown up at the airport for the flight.

Probably far too busy sleeping off a hangover with one of his many girlfriends.

Jamilla cut off the thought, which had conjured up an unhelpful image of the man in front of her stark naked.

'Dane Jones,' he added by way of introduction, while she stood there speechless. Why couldn't she talk right now? 'If you're the welcoming committee, let's go. It's like a damn oven out here.'

'Your... Your Highness,' she began, finally managing to ease a word out of her bone-dry throat. 'I am Jamilla Omar Roussel...' She began the spiel she'd rehearsed. 'I've been assigned as your top diplomatic aide and advisor during your tenure as Zafar's head of state for the European tour and trade mission. Let me introduce you to...' She lifted her arm to indicate the line of dignitaries who had been waiting in the hot sun for far too long and looked stiff with expectation. Before she could remember any of their names, her mind a fuzzy mess, though, he interrupted her.

'Your what, now?' he asked.

'Excuse me?' She dropped her leaden arm.

'What did you just call me?' he asked, a muscle ticking in the stubble on his jawline.

'Your Highness… Your Highness,' she replied.

He sighed, pulling off the cap, and swept his fingers through the mass of wavy hair. 'Yeah, I thought so. Don't.'

'Don't what, Your Highness?' she said, having lost the thread of the conversation, her mind turning to mush under the wave of displeasure rolling off him.

'Don't call me that,' he said, then muttered something under his breath that she felt sure was not polite. 'I'm a US citizen. I answer to my name; that's it. So call me Dane, or Jones, or don't call me anything at all…'

'But, Your Highness, you are a direct blood descendant of the house of Al Amari Khan and second in line to the Zafar throne after Crown Prince Hasan…' she began, the hot weight jammed between her legs joined by a flare of heat in her cheeks.

'Yeah, I get that—' he interrupted her again '—or I wouldn't have had to fly eight thousand miles to this godforsaken…' He cut off the words, but she heard the sentiment and the snap of temper. And her own temper—which had been ruthlessly controlled—snapped back.

Why was he so annoyed? What he had been asked to do was an honour of the highest order. And Zafar wasn't godforsaken. Quite the contrary; it was blessed. Especially since Karim had gained the throne five years ago and begun a bold quest to turn the country back into a constitutional monarchy after his father's disastrous rule, and bring its depleted infrastructure into the twenty-first century.

'I'm doing this for my brother and his wife, end of.' He cut into her thoughts, the snap of anger slicing through her composure. 'He asked me, so I came,' he added, not sounding at all happy about it. 'At considerable expense and inconvenience to me and my business. I had to move a ton of stuff around and bump two major openings into the summer. Here's hoping when we're through, Karim and his cute wife will have two more healthy kids to add to their brood, so I'll be so far down the line of succession no one will ever ask me to do something like this again. But I'm not happy about it. I'm not royal, and I could not give a damn about this country or its future. My life is in New York. So calling me Your Highness is just gonna piss me off more. Okay? So don't do it. Because you won't like me much when I'm pissed.'

'I don't like you much now.'

Did I just say that out loud?

Shock came first, swiftly followed by horror. As her caustic comment echoed across the desert floor, shooting past Dane Jones's tall, indomitable frame and the stunned dignitaries, then echoed around the gleaming jet, the line of chauffeur-driven limos, the grey airport building and boomed out over the inhospitable terrain towards the Palace of the Kings two hours' drive away and probably as far as the Kholadi tribal lands two hundred miles to the north and the neighbouring kingdom of Narabia six hundred miles to the east.

A curse word her mother would have soundly slapped her for even knowing let alone thinking crossed Jamilla's fevered brain—she bit into her lip to stop it bursting out into the fetid, febrile air too.

'I beg your pardon, Your Highness,' she managed, wanting to die on the spot. Or at the very least melt into the puddle which had been forming at her feet.

He didn't say anything. But she could feel that hot, searing gaze on every inch of her skin, making her heart pound hard enough to be heard in Narabia too. The nausea turned the giant knots in her stomach into enormous hanks of rope.

She couldn't believe it. She'd torpedoed the career opportunity of a lifetime—less than two minutes after meeting him. He would have her

replaced. Of course he would. He was a king—
or, rather, a king's brother—and she was supposed to be guiding him through this assignment
with tact and diplomacy, not telling him what
she actually thought of him.

She waited for the axe to fall, busy reconfig-
uring her once stunning resumé in her head,
aware of the horrified looks being sent her way
by the ruling council members and the other
dignitaries. But, just as a wave of panic threatened to engulf her whole body, Dane Jones
yanked off his sunglasses, revealing the most
piercing blue eyes she had ever seen in her life.
A spark twinkled in the deep cerulean blue, the
tanned skin around his eyes crinkled as his gaze
narrowed and she got the impression he was seeing her properly for the first time.

Then he threw back his head and roared with
laughter.

Dane Jones's belly hurt he was laughing so hard.

Damn, but the look on the woman's face had
been priceless as her snapped comment cut
through the desert air as if she'd used a mega-
phone. That look—seriously horrified—had almost been worth getting woken up at dawn and
forced to fly to this sand hole in the desert. Her
previously pinched lips relaxed to form a perfect
O and her eyes—a stunning shade of amber he'd

only just noticed—widened to the size of dinner plates to consume her whole face.

He scrubbed the heel of his hand under his eyelids, actual tears running down his cheeks as the barks of laughter subsided to dull chuckles.

Okay, man, get a grip. It ain't that hilarious.

The truth was he was just exhausted and on edge, and super pissed that he was, one, having to do this thing for a whole month. And, two, being forced to set foot in a country he had promised never to return to in his lifetime.

The minute the jet had touched down, the weight he'd spent years expelling from his stomach had dropped right back into it again. And started to roll around.

Added to all that, he'd had barely any sleep— last night's inaugural event in the new club he'd opened in a rehabbed pickle factory under the High Line hadn't finished until five in the morning. He'd been woken up an hour later in his loft apartment in the Meatpacking District by the stiff now standing ten feet away staring at them both disapprovingly.

He rubbed his hand across his stomach as he finally got a grip, his abdominal muscles sore now.

'Please excuse me, Your Highness...' she began again.

'No excuse necessary. I was being a horse's ass,' he said.

Her shoulders collapsed with relief. Did she think he was going to get her fired over one snarky—and mostly justifiable—comment?

The last of his laughter died. Yeah, probably. Wasn't that exactly the way his father had always treated his subordinates? Even though his brilliant brother had been in charge for five years, he and his pretty little Irish wife couldn't achieve miracles. No doubt the palace staff were still intimidated by his father's autocratic legacy.

With the panicked look gone, Jamilla Roussel's face relaxed, making him more aware of the smudged make-up under those compelling amber eyes and the sheen of perspiration making her soft brown skin glow.

She looked almost as shattered as he felt.

'But I'm not kidding about the Your Highness stuff,' he added. 'That's gotta stop.'

She nodded. 'Absolutely, Mr Jones,' she said, finally getting the message. 'If that is what you prefer.'

'Call me Dane,' he said, not sure why he was goading her but suddenly keen to establish a working relationship with her. He was stuck with this assignment for the next four weeks—he'd given Karim his word, and as his brother had never asked him for a damn thing before now he knew he couldn't wheedle his way out of this promise, like he had so many others in the past.

'I'm not sure I should be so familiar, Your...'
she began, then caught herself '... Mr Jones.'

She really was stunning, he decided. High
cheekbones, wide eyes the colour of rare gems,
ebony hair, the curling tendrils hanging down
from a ruthless knot which only accentuated
her gravity-defying bone structure—and the
lean curves beneath the tailored suit that he'd
noticed straight off because, hey, he was a guy.

'Jamilla, you just told me how much you don't
like me,' he said, enjoying the way her brows
shot up her forehead at the reminder. 'I think we
can safely say over-familiarity isn't gonna be a
problem between us.'

Although, even as he said it, he could feel
the fizz working through his veins—which was
weird. And also not at all welcome.

He was a guy who always appreciated a good-
looking woman, and this woman was certainly
that, but he didn't appreciate rules and regula-
tions and being told what to do—and that was
literally this woman's job. And he also never
dated women he was in a working relationship
with. Firstly because it was *so* not cool, but
more importantly because it could lead to serious complications when the relationship turned
sour, which always happened sooner for him
than for the women he hooked up with.

But the fizz was still there, annoyingly. And
making its presence felt, especially when she

sighed, and he saw her decide to give it to him straight. What was it about those little glimpses of the woman behind the mask of etiquette and appropriate behaviour that appealed to him so much?

'I just don't feel comfortable using your first name under the circumstances, Mr Jones,' she said. 'Not only are you my employer's brother but you're of royal blood and…'

'Okay, hold up.' He held up his hand, the comment making his temper spike. 'Let's figure out a compromise,' he said, forced to appreciate the irony. She had to be the first woman who had ever struggled to use his given name. Ever since he'd hit puberty, women usually wanted to get way too familiar with him, way too fast.

'How about you call me Jones and drop the Mr, which makes me feel prehistoric?' And he was more than jaded enough already at the thought of the next few weeks—and having to pretend to be someone and something he was not, for the benefit of an institution, and a country, he despised.

She studied him and he could see she didn't like it, but he could also see her suck up her disapproval. That she was so transparent didn't help with the fizz one little bit.

She nodded. 'Okay, if you insist.'

'I insist,' he said, getting an added buzz out

of the fact he could insist and she would have to obey him.

Okay, that was kind of kinky. And not in a good way. Since when had he been into dominance and submission?

What made it even hotter, though, was the knowledge that he doubted any guy could get this woman to submit. Not unless she wanted to.

She lifted her arm again and directed him towards the line of stiffs waiting patiently in the sun. 'Can I introduce you to the rest of the ruling council and the King's household staff, most of whom…?'

'No, thanks,' he said, cutting her off before she could launch into another speech.

Just one look at those guys in their official garb made him shudder, bringing back the few unpleasant memories he had of his old man, and made him a lot more aware of how hot it was in the sun, and how much he just wanted to get the rest of this day over with ASAP.

'I'm sorry?' she began, clearly confused by his refusal to follow the protocol. Yup, they were definitely going to need to work on that.

'I'm dripping sweat here and shattered and I'm not in the mood.' He glanced over at the men, most of whom had to be well into their seventies. 'And they look shattered too. How about we reschedule the introductions for tomorrow, somewhere cool?'

'But…' She seemed totally nonplussed for a moment. And it occurred to him she wasn't a particularly spontaneous person. Why did that just make pulling the rug out from under her more appealing?

'But nothing,' he said, channelling the dominant again just for the hell of it. Maybe he could have some fun with this mess after all. 'I'm the guy in charge here, right? For the next little while.'

She nodded slowly, forced to concede the point. Her wary expression had him swallowing down a chuckle—and a new surge of heat.

Yup, that's right, Jamilla. I'm playing this game by my own rules. Not yours, not theirs and sure as hell not the ones set down by my bastard of a father.

'Then I hereby decree we all get into the fleet of limos over there, whack up the air-con and crash out before we pass out.'

Her jaw tensed but a trickle of sweat worked its way down the side of her face, in direct counterpoint to the mutinous look turning those amber eyes to a rich gold.

She wanted to refuse the direct order. The fire in her expression was somehow even more gorgeous than the slight overbite, the defiant pout on her full lips or those stunning golden eyes, but it was pretty obvious she was as hot and exhausted as the rest of them. Sweat stains the size of Brooklyn did not lie. Plus she'd just admitted he was the boss.

She dipped her head in deference to his wishes, but he could see it was an effort from the stiffness in her neck. And a very nice neck it was too, dark springy tendrils clinging to the sweat accentuating the slender line.

'As you wish, Your… Mr Jones,' she said.

'Just Jones,' he corrected her again.

She gave another stiff nod, then spoke briefly to the assistant behind her, before leading him over to the biggest limo in the line. The red and gold flags attached to the hood waved in the hot desert wind.

'Your Highness.' A young man in traditional robes opened the car door then bowed so low Dane was astonished he didn't fall over.

'Thanks, buddy,' he said, holding onto his irritation.

How did Karim deal with this level of deference twenty-four-seven? Because it was already starting to drive him nuts.

He threw his bag into the car then slid into the wonderfully cool interior.

'I'll ride up front so you can rest, Mr Jones,' his new top aide said briskly as she leant into the car but didn't meet his gaze. 'The drive will take approximately two hours. There are refreshments in the bar in front of you. Is there anything else you require?'

Something wholly inappropriate popped into his head, the fizz of awareness becoming a definite buzz.

Down, boy.

He scowled, no longer amused by the unbidden reaction. Because it was just one more inconvenience in a whole host of them.

'It's Jones. Just Jones,' he barked, his voice harsher than he had intended. 'No mister required, remember, Jamilla? And no, I don't require a thing except not to be disturbed until we get there.'

'As you wish,' she said, in that far too obedient voice which he was now sure was totally passive aggressive.

But it wasn't until the young man had closed the door and he'd relaxed into the cold leather, ready to sleep for a week, that it occurred to him she'd avoided calling him Jones again by not calling him anything at all. Thus getting the last laugh.

Touché, Jamilla. You got me... For now.

A wry smile twisted his lips at the thought of their battle of wills.

At least it would distract him from the foggy exhaustion, the prickle of irritation—and the heavy weight in his stomach caused by the ghosts he was going to be forced to confront in two hours and counting.

CHAPTER TWO

'Ms Roussel, His Highness has gone missing...'

Jamilla tapped the stop button on the treadmill in the palace's gym and waited for the machine to power down, taking in the panicked expression on Hakim's face.

Picking up her towel, she mopped the sweat off her neck. 'What did you say, Hakim?' she asked, fairly sure she couldn't possibly have heard the young valet correctly.

Hakim had been assigned to take care of their new head of state, and she had asked him to check on him at precisely six o'clock this morning. Of course, Hakim wasn't supposed to wake Dane Jones if he was still sleeping— he had looked wiped out when they'd arrived at the palace yesterday evening. So wiped out he hadn't even made any sarcastic comments before he'd skulked off to his suite.

But Jamilla had wanted to know as soon as he woke, so she could prepare their schedule accordingly. Thanks to his decision yesterday not to do any official duties, they had a lot to cram into the next week before the tour began.

'His Highness—he is not in his rooms,' Hakim repeated.

'Are you absolutely sure? Perhaps he was in the bathroom?' This was Hakim's first assignment as a valet; he was eager and smart and conscientious, but he was probably as unprepared for dealing with Dane Jones's unconventional behaviour as the rest of them. She'd already figured out her exciting new challenge was going to be a nightmare—which was why she had decided to hit the palace gym for a vigorous two-mile run on the treadmill this morning before facing him.

The man instinctively seemed to know how to provoke her. Running off any excess aggravation before she had to deal with him again had seemed like a good solution—she did not want a recurrence of that weird melting sensation that had assailed her yesterday—or the insult that had slipped out without warning.

That said, she really hadn't expected him to start causing problems so soon.

'I checked everywhere, Ms Roussel,' Hakim said, his voice rising with panic. 'I had the staff help me search the palace. We couldn't find him anywhere. He has left.'

'He... What?'

Where could he have gone? And how? We're in the middle of a desert!

'What about his security detail? Surely they must know where he is?'

Hakim shook his head. 'They said they are not aware; they are only assigned to him when he leaves his suite, and no one had informed them he was awake yet.'

She stepped off the treadmill, her knees wobbling—and not from her workout. 'Okay, Hakim, don't panic…'

Because I'm doing more than enough of that for both of us.

Had he gone back to Manhattan without telling anyone? Was that even possible?

He'd seemed odd yesterday when they'd driven into the palace courtyard. He'd been stiff and silent, his movements lacking the panther-like grace and relaxed confidence she'd noticed at the airstrip. He hadn't even goaded her, just told her he needed to crash and left. But she'd noticed the muscle in his jaw ticking overtime, and the haunted look in his eyes.

She'd assumed the strained, empty expression was fatigue. Now she wasn't so sure.

She shot towards the gym's shower units, barking orders over her shoulder en route.

'Get Saed to check with the palace guards. Then contact the garage and see if he's taken one of the palace cars.' Every vehicle had a GPS tracker, so there was that. Could he have headed back to the airstrip? Surely not. He couldn't have taken the jet without someone knowing.

Think, Jamilla, think.

'Perhaps he's taken one of the all-terrain vehicles.' Surely that had to be it. If he'd left the palace, maybe he'd just gone for a drive to the nearest town to meet the local people... *Five miles away? Through the desert? Alone?*

Did he have any idea how dangerous the desert could be? How tough the terrain was to navigate? Of course he didn't; he lived a pampered, pointless existence in Manhattan.

And why would he want to meet people he'd already made it clear he had no desire to represent?

'Yes, Ms Roussel,' Hakim said, turning to rush off.

'Wait!'

The young man skidded to a stop. 'Yes, Ms Roussel.'

'Do you know if His Highness can ride a horse?' Was it possible—could he have taken one of Karim's prized Arabians for a ride?

Even the thought of it had her stomach dropping to the floor and her throat contracting. Her breathing accelerated past panic to hyperventilating.

Hakim stared at her. 'Um...'

'It's okay, forget I asked that,' she said, and let Hakim rush off.

What were the chances Dane Jones could ride a horse well enough to handle one of Karim's highly strung thoroughbreds? The Arabians could only be ridden safely by people like herself, who had been riding almost before they could walk. And the desert terrain was even more treacherous on horseback.

But, as she showered and changed, the panic refused to subside. Because she already suspected just how arrogant and reckless their new head of state was.

After getting dressed, she dashed down to the palace stables, just to put her mind at ease while they waited for news. She reassured herself every step of the way that even Jones couldn't be *that* arrogant or *that* reckless—to risk breaking his neck in the middle of nowhere, just to spite her. She was being ridiculous.

Ten minutes later, though, she discovered her gut instinct had been correct.

Dane Jones was even more arrogant and reckless than she could possibly have imagined. And she still had no clue where he'd gone.

Dane let out a rebel yell, the shout lost in the rush of wind and the surge of adrenaline as the horse's muscles worked in fluid motion beneath him and he shot up the rocky dune chasing the red light of the dawn.

He gave the stallion its head, let the animal fly and felt as if he were flying too, away from the energy-sapping fury of being forced to spend a night in the palace again after twenty-five years. He'd had to get out of there, get away. He'd have to go back soon enough and endure another week of the place, to get the job done he'd promised his brother he would do. But at least this dawn ride to the Halu Oasis would make it a little more bearable, a little less draining—bringing back one of the few good memories from his early childhood in Zafar.

As they crested the rocky ridge, Dane squeezed his knees and tugged on the reins. The horse lifted its head and slowed—so expertly trained it only needed the suggestion of an instruction once it had conceded who was boss.

Dane smiled as he patted the horse's neck.

It had been touch and go there for a while, after they'd left the palace, Azzam testing to see if Dane had the skill and strength to handle him. But they'd figured it out in the end and Dane had enjoyed every minute of it. Nothing like a head-to-head with a one-thousand-pound stallion with an attitude problem to clear out the cobwebs after a virtually sleepless night.

The pulse of adrenaline hit hard.

Of course, not all his restlessness had been

down to the overflow of memories from his childhood, he thought ruefully, remembering the dream which had woken him up in a sweaty mess before dawn—featuring wide amber eyes sparking with challenge and the musty scent of girl sweat.

Yeah, not going there, remember?

He ignored the awareness rushing over his skin and concentrated on the twinge in his thigh muscles as the stallion picked its way down the slope towards the water as sure-footed as a cat. It had been a while since he'd been on a horse—probably at least six months since he'd been able to take a break and visit the farm he owned in Upstate New York where he kept his own stables. He'd pay for this ride tomorrow for sure, but as his gaze landed on the cluster of palm trees, the small corral, the sparkle of iridescent blue water bubbling from the fissure in the red rocks, he knew every single ache and pain would be worth it.

Calm settled over him at last. He could remember the feel of his brother's arms around him as he cradled Dane's small body against his bony chest and they rode out to this place—an oasis in more ways than one during the turmoil of their childhoods—to catch the dawn together a million summers ago. He could even hear the ten-year-old Karim—an expert horseman even then—speaking to him in Zafari, patient words of reassurance and encouragement and distraction to stop him crying, back when Dane had been fluent in the language too.

He let out a half laugh, amused by his own sentimentality.

Damn, if Karim knew how much that long-ago memory still meant to him, and how much he'd missed those summer rides, this single spot, once he and his mom had been kicked out of Zafar for good, his brother would probably cough up a lung laughing.

After jumping down from the horse, he pressed his face into the stallion's neck, clung to it for a moment, feeling grounded again for the first time since he'd agreed to this fiasco. He stroked the sleek coat, took in a lungful of the pungent scent of horse sweat and grinned. 'Good boy, Azzam.'

The horse snorted and whinnied, acknowledging the compliment as if it were his due. The animal really was magnificent. No surprise there, though. Karim had always been a connoisseur of prime horseflesh.

He led the stallion into the corral, glad to see the place was still kept well stocked. The burble from the waterfall was almost musical in the desert quiet as the morning sunshine made its presence felt. The water beckoned, cool and clear, a translucent turquoise he'd never seen anywhere else, as he filled up the horse's water pouch. A swim would be the perfect way to wash off the layer of sweat and grit he'd accumulated during the hard ride, before he had to head back. But he unsaddled the horse first, took off its bridle, rubbed it down, cleaned its hooves, then fed and watered it—just the way his big brother had taught him a lifetime ago.

Jamilla drove along the rocky ridge, following the trail she'd managed to pick up just outside the palace grounds nearly an hour ago. Her skills as a tracker were rusty, but it hadn't been that hard to follow the trail of turned rocks, crushed plants, the occasional hoof print, given that the horse and rider had clearly been moving at speed. Once she'd realised how fast Dane Jones was travelling on Karim's prize stallion she'd had several anxiety attacks. Had the horse bolted? It must have. It was a miracle she hadn't found the man's broken body already. She'd contacted the palace guards on the satellite phone she had in her pack, told them to meet her with an ambulance at the trail head just in case, once she'd figured out the horse seemed to be heading towards the Halu Oasis.

Her head lifted as the scent of fresh water hit her nostrils. The Jeep topped the last rise and Jamilla scanned what she could see of the pool and its surrounds from the dune. She spotted Karim's stallion Azzam, unsaddled, standing sedately in the shaded corral eating from a feed bag as she drove up to the fence. But there was no sign of the man.

She jumped out of the Jeep. As she rounded the small shelter she noticed someone had filled the trough with water for the stallion and taken off his saddle and bridle.

Dane. Not dead then. Safe. By some miracle.

The anxiety finally released its stranglehold on her throat. Fury replaced the panic. By an incredible stroke of luck he'd survived the ride, while sending her and the whole of the palace staff into an uproar. She had helicopters out scouring the area, three all-terrain vehicles heading in opposite directions from hers, just in case the trail she'd found wasn't his.

She heard the splash of water and headed through the grove of desert scrub and palm trees, determined to find him and give him a piece of her mind. She didn't care if he was Zafar's head of state for the next month, she didn't care if he was Karim's half-brother and second in line to the throne, she didn't even care any more that she was effectively his subordinate. She wanted to murder him with her bare hands—for putting himself and Azzam in danger, for wasting everyone's time, and for scaring the life out of her.

Of all the arrogant, reckless, thoughtless...

But as she stepped from the cover of the

palms and reached the pool's edge, the heated diatribe in her head cut off and heat exploded into her cheeks.

A man stood not twenty feet away, with his back to her under the fall of water from the rocks.

A completely naked man, the muscles of his spine, his long legs and impossibly broad shoulders glistening in the sunshine as the water pounded down.

He moved, reaching up to slick back his hair and tilt his face into the deluge. Her avid gaze skimmed over him, taking in every stunning detail. The red and black tattoo that covered his right shoulder and most of his upper arm, another scrawled across the bottom of his back, just above the tight, hard, perfectly formed muscles of his glutes. Sensation—hot, fluid, devastating—flared across her sweaty skin like wildfire under her short robe, heating the burning in her cheeks and flowing like hot lava to lodge between her thighs.

The fury she wanted to feel was replaced by shock. And stunned arousal.

She shouldn't spy on him. He was still a prince and not someone she needed to know intimately, in any way.

So look away then.

But she couldn't stop her hungry gaze from devouring every inch of his bronzed skin. The lighter patch across his buttocks, the ink old and new, the small scars on his back, his shoulder, that suggested a life not quite as pampered as she'd assumed.

She was utterly spellbound.

She'd never seen a naked man before in the flesh. And certainly not one in his prime. She'd seen pictures in textbooks, of course she had. She was twenty-four years old and she'd always been curious about sex. Excited about finding the right guy—once she'd established her career—to experiment with. She'd had kisses, even a bit more than that while studying in Narabia; she wasn't a prude. And she didn't feel the need to wait for marriage, as so many young women her age did in Zafar. Her mother had eloped with a French diplomat as a nineteen-year-old, having rejected the arranged marriage her parents had wanted. While that hasty marriage had ended up being a disaster, Farah Omar had always had a forthright view of sex, which she'd passed on to her daughter.

Jamilla had told herself she just hadn't found the right guy yet—to go the whole way with. But neither had she felt the yearning to search for him… Until now.

She swallowed heavily, the insistent throbbing between her legs beginning to ache. She had never expected to feel something so raw and real and… Insistent.

Except Dane Jones is not the right guy. Not even close. You don't even like him.

Despite her best efforts, though, her gaze remained riveted to his physique as he turned and strolled back towards her, his head bent to avoid stepping on the sharper rocks on the pool bed.

Her gaze dipped past the ripple of muscle and sinew, glittering in the sunlight, to locate another tattoo scrawled across his hip flexor, before zeroing in on the long column of his sex nestled in dark hair. Her throat dried to parchment and moisture flooded her core. Her knees shook and her eyes felt as if they were about to bug right out of her head.

And everything flew out of her head, bar one singular, astonishing and terrifying thought.

He's absolutely beautiful.

Dane's head lifted, alerted by the sound of a gasp so loud he could hear it above the splashing waterfall. He stopped, spotting the striking young woman standing on the bank. She wore a voluminous thigh-length robe which covered her head and gathered around her waist in the hot desert breeze, doing nothing to disguise her athletic build and the shape of high full breasts. His gaze took in the jeans and boots which completed the arresting picture.

She was stunning. He was stark naked and

she was staring straight at his… The swell of arousal hit hard.

Who was she? What was she doing here? And did she like what she saw, because he sure as hell did. Maybe they could…?

But then her head lifted, their gazes met, and he recognised those amber eyes—dazed with shocked awareness.

Hell, it's just Jamilla. My royal babysitter.

Irritation and something which felt vaguely like disappointment joined the shot of heat which refused to die.

Damn, did Little Miss Protocol follow me here?

He kept walking, satisfied when her gaze jerked away from his junk at last, and began to study the bushes to her left as if her life depended on it.

'How about you throw me my shorts?' he said, vindicated by the fierce flush on her cheeks.

If you didn't want to see it, honey, you shouldn't have looked.

'You're staring right at them,' he added, because she seemed to be frozen in place.

She cleared her throat. 'Um… Yes.' Jolted out of her trance, she scrambled to find his boxers among the pile of clothing he'd left on the bush. She threw them towards him, then turned her back on him. 'I apologise for…for…' She seemed at a loss for words, and because he was having difficulty controlling his reaction to her heated stare he decided to help her out.

'For checking out my junk?'

Her head swung round, then swung straight back again when she caught him still tugging on his shorts. But he'd spotted the flash of temper and it was almost as enjoyable as the now nuclear blush.

'I—I didn't expect... I mean, I—I didn't mean to...' she stammered, struggling to explain.

Sure you did. A blush that radioactive doesn't lie.

'It's okay, Jamilla. You're not the first woman to see me naked,' he said, unable to resist the chance for some payback. After all, he was struggling to control an inconvenient erection, and she was the cause. 'Luckily, I'm not a shy guy.'

'Well, that's fairly obvious,' she murmured.

He laughed. He couldn't help it. Her hissed comment was almost as hot as the sight of her standing on the bank like a young Valkyrie checking him out.

He leant past her to grab his T-shirt, felt her stiffen and shift away.

'Relax,' he said. 'You're not my type.'

But, even as he said it, he captured a lungful of her musky scent—fresh and spicy, overlaid with a tinge of salty sweat—and knew it was a lie.

The truth was he'd never considered himself to even have a type. All he required of hook-ups was that they be available, uncomplicated and into him. If that was a type, this woman was the opposite of all his main requirements. But there was something about her that got to him. Maybe it was the fierce intelligence he sensed behind the veneer of deference, maybe it was those compelling hints of temper he seemed able to trigger despite her best efforts to keep them hidden, maybe it was just that she was insanely gorgeous in an artless, unstudied, vaguely uptight way. Maybe it was the challenge she represented—or maybe it was a combination of all those things. But whatever the hell it was about her that made him want to tease and provoke her and see the flash of gold light up her eyes—he didn't like it. Because he preferred his sex life to be simple. And Jamilla Roussel had complication written all over her.

Perhaps this was just the result of not having any woman in his bed for months—an enforced drought brought about by the success of his business, and the fact he'd become jaded with the whole dating scene in recent years. Given his current circumstances, he wasn't going to be able to remedy that situation for at least another four weeks.

Awesome!

'That's very good news,' she said, protesting

way too much as the wind whipped the scarf off her head, revealing her long dark hair, ruthlessly tied into a bunch. 'It would be completely inappropriate and make our working relationship untenable. I have a…'

Her prim statement faded away as the rush of blood heading south gathered pace. He rubbed his T-shirt across his pecs, his gaze snagging on her slender neck.

What would she taste like in the soft hollow beneath her earlobe? Sweet? Spicy? Even a little sour? How would she react if he nuzzled the smooth skin? Would she giggle? Gasp? Moan?

Not gonna happen. Not your type, buddy, remember?

He tugged the damp T-shirt over his head, grabbed his jeans, trying to control the new blast of heat.

'How did you find me?' he demanded, interrupting whatever she'd been saying about their working relationship. Not that they had one. Not one that was working at any rate.

'Can I turn around?' she asked, sounding a little more sure of herself again. 'Are you decent?'

'*Decent?*' He chuckled. 'No one's ever accused me of that.'

She huffed. 'I meant are you fully clothed, Mr Jones?'

Again with the mister.

He shrugged. 'Sure.' She turned to face him and he noticed the blush had become less explosive. Shame, the colour added a becoming glow to her tawny skin. 'You really oughta call me Dane, seeing as you've seen more of me now than some women I've slept with.'

The blush reignited. And her brows crinkled into a cute frown. 'Okay, *Dane*,' she murmured, and he gave himself a mental high five—knowing he'd just scored a major victory in their battle of wills.

'In answer to your question, I followed your trail in one of the palace Jeeps, which wasn't that difficult as you were obviously going so fast,' she said. 'I was extremely worried about your safety after I heard you'd taken Azzam for a ride.'

'Uh-huh,' he said, impressed she'd managed to track him, and also weirdly touched by the genuine concern in her tone.

No one had ever been worried about his safety before. Not even his mom. Not *ever* his mom.

'Well, I survived,' he said, annoyed now by the pulse of reaction caused by her worried frown.

'You don't seem to understand, the Arabians are very temperamental, Dane. Azzam in particular needs a really experienced rider. You could have been thrown.' The schoolmarm tone was back. And while a part of him found that

haughty attitude a major turn-on—*go, figure*—
another part of him found it super annoying.

'Not only that, but you're very lucky to have
stumbled upon this oasis.' She huffed and
crossed her arms over her chest, which plumped
up her spectacular breasts.

Terrific.

'Uh-huh,' he said again, as it occurred to him
she hadn't just underestimated his ability to control Azzam. She'd also assumed he was dumb
as a post.

'The desert can be an extremely unforgiving
environment for the unwary, Dane,' she added,
condescension dripping from every word now,
her frown becoming a lot less cute. 'Or the unprepared.'

Clearly, they were going to have to get a few
things straight before they went any further.

'I didn't luck onto this oasis,' he said, letting
his irritation show—as the buzz of arousal flowing south started to piss him off.

What was it about her that got him hot and
mad at the same time? Because that was just
perverse.

'I knew exactly where I was going. In fact,
I could probably find this place blindfolded
if I had to, because it's the only place in this
whole godforsaken country that doesn't give
me nightmares. And FYI, I've been riding
since I was three years old—and Azzam is a

smart horse—smart enough to figure out real quick who's the boss.'

She blinked and dropped her arms—the hissy stance gone. But something else had replaced it, something he liked even less. Why was she looking at him with that strange emotion in her eyes? As if he'd revealed something he hadn't intended?

'*You,* on the other hand…?' he said, determined to push back against it.

Satisfaction surged when the blush went radioactive again.

'I see. I'm sorry for the misunderstanding.' But then she looked at him as if she did understand.

He should have won that round, so why did he feel as if he hadn't? Quite.

'Are you ready to return to the palace?' she asked.

Not ever.

'Sure.' He wasn't a quitter, not any more.

But when they got back to the corral and he saddled his horse, he soon discovered they had another problem. One that didn't improve his mood one little bit.

'I can call on the satellite phone and have one of the palace mechanics pick me up,' Jamilla said, already reaching for her pack. She should have checked the Jeep was properly equipped before she'd left the palace, but she'd been frantic. And now the vehicle had a flat tyre and no spare.

'How long will that take?' he asked.

'Not long,' she said, feeling like a fool.

She'd miscalculated, badly. Dane Jones wasn't the pampered playboy she'd assumed. The scars and the haunted look when he spoke of his memories of Zafar, suggested a very different reality. Why hadn't she researched his past properly? She had assumed he would have no memory of his homeland. He'd left when he was still a young boy and never returned. Because he was his father's second child, the product of the King's disastrous fourth marriage, and Karim had been the Crown Prince, by all accounts Sheikh Abdullah had not maintained contact with the boy or his mother after the divorce. But from the darkness in Dane Jones's gaze, the flash of turmoil, and the memory of his reaction yesterday when they had arrived at the Palace of the Kings—surly and tense—she could see now Jones's past association with Zafar might well be more traumatic than she had assumed.

She knew from intimate conversations with Orla, who had become a friend as well as her employer over the last five years, that Karim's childhood had been blighted by Abdullah's violence towards his mother. What if Dane had experienced something similar? Compassion welled in her throat. She needed to speak to

Saed and maybe Ameera—who had attended King Abdullah's wives at the Palace.

If she was going to do her job properly, she needed to understand where Dane Jones was coming from. She had to earn his trust. She had assumed he was arrogant, but it appeared she was the arrogant one who had not done her job properly.

'How long?' he demanded again.

'An hour, maybe two,' she replied. It would serve her right for driving out here without doing the proper research about Dane Jones's ability in the saddle.

The thought brought with it an unbidden image of him walking from the water with all the grace and strength of a sea god, gloriously naked, and not at all pleased to see her standing there like a ninny, gaping at him.

Getting stranded at the oasis would serve her right for that piece of unconscionable voyeurism too.

She found the satellite phone at last, the heat burning the back of her neck as well as her cheeks.

'Figures,' he grunted and strode off to saddle his horse.

After she finished calling through the problem to the palace garage and letting them know to call off the search party, Jamilla watched as Dane grabbed the pommel of his saddle and

mounted the powerful black stallion in one
fluid move.

Azzam snorted indignantly, then reared.

Jamilla braced for Dane to fall off, panic
shooting through her. But he controlled the
horse effortlessly with light touches on the reins,
his commands calm and steady but firm, his
body at one with the huge animal, utterly un-
fazed by the stallion's fit of pique.

The man, like the horse, looked magnificent—every inch the desert prince despite the
jeans and baseball cap, even if he didn't think
of himself as one.

Jamilla's breath released, the shame wash-
ing over her again. Whatever happened next,
this man deserved her respect. He had returned
to a country that held few happy memories for
him at his brother's request. And while she had
originally resented the need to have him lead
this diplomatic mission, they were both stuck
with this situation.

The horse settled down quickly, Dane's easy
mastery making Jamilla feel like even more of a
clueless idiot. His expert horsemanship also am-
plified the pulse in her abdomen, which hadn't
left her since she'd first spotted him in the water.

Another fitting penance for your hubris.

She vowed never to underestimate him again.
Or the catastrophic effect he seemed to have on
her hormones.

'Have you called in the breakdown?' he asked.

She nodded, a little perturbed when he trotted towards her on the horse. Leaning forward, he extended his hand. 'Come on,' he beckoned. 'We can double up. I'm not leaving you alone out here for hours in the middle of the day.'

She stepped back instinctively, disturbed as much by his gruff chivalry as she was at the thought of sharing a saddle with him all the way back to the palace.

'It's okay, there's water here and shade. I can easily…'

'Jamilla, that's an order,' he said, but then his lips twisted in a mocking smile, the challenge in his eyes unmistakable. 'I promise not to bite. And I'm sure you've got a ton of things we need to be doing today.'

It was a dare. Plain and simple. A dare she had to take or he'd know how the sight of him naked was still playing havoc with her senses.

'Okay, thanks,' she murmured, not feeling remotely thankful.

She clasped his forearm. A zap of electricity shot through her as he gripped her arm and the calluses on his palm rubbed her skin. He yanked her up behind him with an effortless strength which had the weight in her stomach plummeting further south.

She sank into the saddle, jammed up against him, her thighs cupping his muscular butt and the scent of fresh water, musty horse and salty male sweat suffocating her. She eased back, trying to create some distance between her chest and his back. Maybe if she could just...

'You're gonna need to hold on, Jamilla,' he said, interrupting her desperate thoughts. Resting one large hand on her knee, he gave it a condescending pat. 'Or this trip will take even longer. And I've got a feeling neither one of us wants that.'

True.

She let go of the saddle and banded her arms around his waist, pressing her face into his back. Her nipples swelled into stiff peaks on contact—because, of course they did.

Please don't let him be able to feel them.

He pressed his heels into the horse's flanks and flicked the reins over its neck. 'Let's go, boy.'

The stallion launched into a gallop, forcing Jamilla to tighten her grip and cling to his strong, powerful body.

She ground her teeth together and squeezed her eyes shut, her body acutely aware of every flex and bulge of his as they flew towards the dunes.

Then she prayed, as she'd never prayed before, that she would survive the next hour of pure, unadulterated—and totally deserved—torture.

CHAPTER THREE

'JAMILLA, ARE YOU busy? I have something for you to see.'

Jamilla looked up from her laptop to see Saed Khouri, the head of the royal household, standing at the door to her office with a file folder under his arm.

Of course I'm busy. The tour starts tomorrow. And I'm not sure Dane Jones will ever be comfortable as a royal representative.

She cut off the unhelpful panicked thought and took a breath before closing her laptop.

'Of course, come in, Saed.' She glanced at her watch. Ten o'clock already; she should try to clock off before midnight. The royal entourage was scheduled to leave for Rome at nine in the morning—and she wanted to be as fresh as she could be.

She needed to be able to keep her wits about her at all times if she was going to be travelling so closely with Dane.

That said, she and Dane had somehow managed to create a stable working relationship in the last seven days. Ever since their torturous ride back from the oasis he had even been co-operative…mostly.

It was obvious he found the whole concept of monarchy a challenge. But she'd learned to live with the tension between them, tried to forget what she'd seen at the oasis, and had managed to maintain a professional—or professional enough—demeanour ever since. And so had he.

While she'd briefed him extensively on the punishing schedule they had committed to over the next three weeks, he'd sat patiently without much comment. She suspected it was because he was bored, but she had considered it a major boon he had managed to refrain from any sarcastic remarks.

It seemed they'd both returned from the oasis with a greater respect for each other and she was certainly a great deal more aware of her dangerous attraction to him—and the pressing need to control it. She had decided work was the perfect solution to the problem.

With that in mind, she'd worked tirelessly during the time she had away from him—while he was dealing with his own business concerns—to refine those events that were flexible over the next three weeks during their whistle-stop tour of key EU countries where Zafar was looking to increase its trading links.

Originally planned for Karim and Orla—who had a great deal more experience of the role required of Zafar's royal ambassadors—the European tour had included events which would not play to Dane's strengths or interests. So, liaising with all the relevant authorities, Jamilla had managed to modify some elements of the itinerary she thought might be particularly challenging for him—the day-long visit to an all-girls academy in Barcelona, for example, which had fitted perfectly with Orla's passion for female education, had been reduced to two hours. Forcing Dane Jones to spend a whole day with a group of pubescent girls had seemed like a recipe for disaster; she could just imagine every one of them developing an inappropriate crush on him.

Her face heated. After all, he seemed to have that effect on a lot of women.

With some careful juggling, she'd also managed to factor in a two-day stopover in County Kildare to visit Karim and Orla after their first week in Italy, sure that a chat with his brother couldn't help but bolster Dane's confidence.

Not that Dane Jones seemed lacking in confidence, generally speaking. Quite the opposite. But she couldn't seem to dismiss the shadows in his eyes when he had first arrived at the palace, and when he'd spoken of his past experience of Zafar at the oasis. They hadn't talked of the oasis since, and she could only be grateful for that too. Because she was very much afraid she had the vision of him naked coming out of that pool tattooed on her retinas for all eternity— and, along with all the work she was doing, it wasn't helping with her sleep deprivation.

The duties Dane would be carrying out, though, were going to be exceptionally challenging for him—not least because he had no knowledge whatsoever of Zafar's people and culture as it was now. So, as well as all the briefings— and her own efforts to tailor the schedule better for Dane—Jamilla had also arranged a series of visits with him to local clinics and schools, the nearby marketplace and a string of businesses, ostensibly to give him some hands-on training in royal protocol, but also to introduce him to his countrymen and women and the modern desert kingdom he would be representing.

She'd congratulated herself on the hands-on approach; at least he hadn't seemed bored— she'd also discovered he understood a great deal more Zafari than he'd let on, even if he said he didn't speak the language. Underneath the bored, jaded cynic, Dane was a people person— unconventional, yes, but also compelling, a man who could be very charismatic if he wanted to be—which had to explain why his nightclub empire was such a success. She planned to build on those strengths as much as she could, while at the same time ensuring she didn't make the mistake of falling under his spell herself.

Luckily, so far, he seemed determined not to turn his killer charm on her, which could only be a good thing.

'Come in, Saed. What's on your mind?' she asked as the head of household continued to hover by the door.

She and Saed had not always seen eye to eye. He'd struggled to accept a woman in the new role of chief diplomatic aide, but while he was a traditionalist, she knew he was also extremely good at his job. She'd spoken to him about Dane's childhood in the palace, but Saed had said he had no information he could share. As it was over twenty-five years ago, she had understood. Similarly Ameera—the Queen's principal lady-in-waiting—had told her she knew nothing about King Abdullah's marriage to Kitty Jones as the American socialite had brought her own employees to the palace with her and had spent most of the five-year marriage out of the kingdom—jetting back to America and Europe and only taking her son with her to the US after the divorce. Which had seemed strange and rather sad to Jamilla—why hadn't Dane's mother taken her young son with her when she'd travelled? But Jamilla hadn't been able to glean any more information and had decided not to pursue it further.

Now she and Dane seemed to have established a workable relationship, perhaps it would be best for her not to risk disturbing it by probing into his past.

Saed nodded and walked into the room, placing the file folder on the desk. It was older than she had assumed, faded and crammed with what looked like correspondence.

'After our conversation about His Highness, I decided to look back through His Majesty King Abdullah's personal effects,' Saed said. 'I was sure I had seen something there that might be of interest… This evening I found the file I was looking for.'

'Oh, I see.' She studied the folder, her curiosity piqued. 'What's in here?' she asked, pulling the folder towards her and flipping it open, but before Saed answered she could see what the correspondence was. The address on the first letter—which simply said *The King, Zafar Palace*—was written in a child's hand with a New York postmark. She flipped the letter over and found a return address also written in a child's hand.

Dane Amari Khan
Centil Parc West
USA
The World

So he hadn't always refused to use his father's name.

'They are letters—many letters,' Saed said. 'From the young Prince to his father, written over a period of six years, after he left Zafar with his mother.'

Jamilla swallowed past the raw spot forming in her throat. Every one of the letters, she noted, was unopened.

'Do you know if King Abdullah received them?' Surely he couldn't have. If he had, wouldn't he have opened them? Or at least had his staff open them?

'They were with his personal effects, so I believe he must have,' Saed said, his voice low with concern.

She realised from the grave look on Saed's face that the austere head of household must have realised the implication too. King Abdullah had made a point of not opening his second son's letters. Of filing them away and ignoring them. But he had kept them too, making the decision not to open them seem even more callous and vindictive.

She sighed and ran her thumb over the painstakingly written address on the first letter, from a child who had probably only recently learned how to write.

Perhaps she should have expected this. She knew King Abdullah had been a difficult and controlling man. He had abused at least one of his wives, Karim's mother, Cassandra Wainwright, and been violent towards Karim when he was a teenager and he had returned to Zafar during the summers, having him whipped whenever he defied his father. But why did this feel even more cruel and neglectful?

She flicked through the letters, noticed the handwriting becoming more fluid, more cursive as Dane became older, the return address changing frequently, but also becoming more accurate and better spelt. Each envelope, though, remained sealed.

Nausea joined the sadness pressing on her chest, the strange feeling of connection unbidden, but there nonetheless. She knew what it was like to be rejected by your father, after all.

'Do you wish to open them?' Saed asked. 'Perhaps, if you read them, you would get the picture you seek of His Highness's relationship with his father.'

Probably, but she knew she couldn't open them or read them, however curious she was about the content. She had no right.

She shook her head. 'Thanks for these, Saed. I think the right thing to do is probably to return them to Dane.'

She hated to be the one to do that. Hated that his father's behaviour probably wouldn't dispose him to think well of the Zafari monarchy, the legacy he was here to represent or her either, by association. Discovering that his father had never opened the letters he'd sent him would also risk undoing all her efforts in the past week to get him more invested in the country and the culture that was his birthright.

But what else could she do? Surely the little boy who had written to his father so diligently over so many years, and probably waited just as diligently for a reply, had a right to know the truth.

CHAPTER FOUR

DANE STEPPED OUT of the chauffeur-driven limo at Zafar's airstrip to find Jamilla waiting at the bottom of the aeroplane steps. Awareness shot through him as he took in her athletic frame in the fitted pant suit, the colourful headscarf whipping around her face.

Her gaze fixed on his and he felt the reaction everywhere, damn her.

She was a beautiful woman, no doubt about it. But why couldn't he get a grip on his reaction to her? Why couldn't he get those amber eyes, those sleek curves out of his dreams? They'd been working together pretty closely in the last week and he'd made sure to keep things professional, but his awareness of her had only become more intense. And it was starting to make him surly, which he knew wasn't fair. He'd seen the adjustments she'd made to the tour itinerary, knew she'd worked her butt off to help him out. And he appreciated it. But why did she have to look so hot in her tailored suits and pristine hair and make-up?

Still off-limits, buddy.

'Hi Dane, did Hakim forget to provide your uniform this morning?' she asked.

'I told Hakim to put it in my luggage,' he said. Or, rather, snapped.

He drew in a breath but resisted the urge to apologise when she stiffened at his tone. Yeah, maybe it wasn't her fault she affected him in this way, but the clothes were an issue. After spending some time in the last few days getting fitted for what he had assumed would be something more formal to wear to the balls they had scheduled, Hakim had laid out a made-to-measure Zafari dress uniform this morning for him to travel in—complete with gold epaulettes, brass buttons and a row of ribbons he hadn't earned—and he wasn't happy. Why the heck did he have to dress like a soldier when he had never served in the Zafari army—and certainly was not its honorary commander-in-chief like his brother?

'We need to talk about what I'm wearing and when. Because I'm not comfortable in that outfit.'

'I see,' she said carefully, which only pissed him off more. While their working relationship had been less tense in the last few days, he missed the spitfire he'd glimpsed in the early days. Maybe it was just that his temper wanted company. But he didn't like wearing masks and he wasn't comfortable with her wearing one either.

He followed her up the steps and into the jet, far too aware of how her fitted pants accentuated her trim butt.

Look away from the booty.

As they entered the main cabin area—the air crew doing that dipping bow as he passed, which he hated—he caught a whiff of Jamilla's scent, reminding him of the return journey from the oasis. The memory of that ride was still waking him up at night—hot and sweaty and ready to explode.

'What is the problem with the uniform?' she asked as they sat, her face a picture of puzzled concern.

'Are you kidding me?' he asked. 'I'm not wearing it; I'd feel like a phoney.' Or, worse, he'd look like his father.

'But the uniform of the commander-in-chief is a ceremonial one worn by the head of state, an honour bestowed on the Kings of Zafar for generations.'

'I'm not the King,' he cut in bluntly.

'Perhaps we could compromise,' she offered.

'How?' he said, not feeling flexible, the light flush on her cheeks reminding him of how she'd looked while checking out his...

Not going there, Jones, remember?

'Would you be prepared to wear the uniform for the state balls and banquets you have to attend at least? Such as the one being given at the Ambassador's residence in Paris?'

He supposed he could live with that, but her concerted efforts to placate him were only making him feel more taciturn and surly. He knew it was her job to make sure he was appropriately attired, but he didn't like being treated as if he were some unruly kid who needed to be managed. Especially by her.

'You would not look out of place,' she said, the patient tone not helping with his irritation. 'Everyone there will be wearing tuxedos or uniforms and traditional ceremonial wear.'

'Uh-huh… What are you going to be wearing?'

She blinked again, the flush brightening. 'I have a suit to wear to the event.'

'Like the one you're wearing now?'

'Um…yes. I will be working in the background. I'm not actually attending the ball as a guest but as part of the royal entourage.'

She looked flustered, which gave him an idea—an idea which would no doubt shock her, but he decided to go with it—because it was already taking the edge off his bad mood. 'I'm not going to that ball on my own, Jamilla. End of. And I'm sure as hell not going to it in that uniform without you right there beside me in something equally OTT.' He thought for a minute. 'Like a ball gown.'

'I don't understand,' she said, the stunned look starting to amuse him. She was cute when she was caught outside her comfort zone. Who knew?

'Okay, I'll spell it out for you. If you want me to go to the ball in that outfit, you're going as my date.' He had never seen her in anything other than those severe pant suits or the jeans she'd worn at the oasis. What was wrong with wanting to see her in a dress, something sleek and sexy to match her colouring and those amber eyes? It would probably increase his torture but he didn't care, because this wasn't just about the clothes any more, he realised. He didn't want her in the background; he wanted her beside him, especially for the big state occasions.

He knew how to work a crowd but he was not comfortable in the role of head of state, and he was even less comfortable representing Zafar. He didn't want to screw up this assignment. And not just because he'd made a promise to his brother.

In the last week, after touring the country to get him into the role of fake King, he'd met a lot of people. Smart, hard-working, loyal citizens who looked up to the Zafari monarchy.

He wanted to get this right, for them as well as his brother and Orla, but that still wasn't going to make him a natural at this job. Having Jamilla there—smiling whenever he did something right and making quick constructive comments when he messed up—would provide some much-needed backup.

Plus she fascinated him and entertained him, despite the awareness he didn't seem able to shake.

'But I can't go as your date. It wouldn't be appropriate,' she said, looking horrified now.

'Take it or leave it,' he said. 'Those are my terms. Either that or I'll wear what I'm comfortable in.' Truth was, he had a couple of tuxedos which he could have flown over, but she didn't need to know that.

She simply stared—probably assuming he was planning to turn up at the Zafari ambassador's residence in Paris wearing ripped jeans and a T. He had to hold back a wry smile, but then she chewed on her bottom lip, which sent an uncomfortable shot of adrenaline to his groin.

Eventually she huffed, 'I suppose I could speak to their Majesties when we arrive in County Kildare. If they are okay with the break in protocol, I might be able to borrow something from Orla to accompany you to the ambassador's ball in Paris. If you're sure that's what you want?'

'Positive,' he said, the surge of triumph enhancing the surge of awareness.

Who knew? Calling her bluff was almost as hot as watching her bite into that full bottom lip.

He'd be playing with fire; he knew that. He'd seen the way she stared at him when she thought he wasn't looking. He could still remember the longing in her eyes when he'd caught her sizing him up naked at the oasis. And he could still feel her nipples poking him in the back like a couple of torpedoes ready to launch as they rode back to the palace.

The memories of that ride had woken him up hard and ready every night since. But as he relaxed into his seat and she headed off to speak to the crew before take-off, the usual spike of irritation didn't come.

Maybe this trip didn't have to be such a chore after all. He'd tried ignoring his attraction to Jamilla and it hadn't worked. Sure, keeping her close was going to be pure torture, but torture was better than boredom.

Not only that, but challenging her, provoking her and coaxing out that rebellious streak she kept hidden under the veneer of protocol might help control the brutal twist of inadequacy and the dark thoughts that had haunted him ever since he had returned to Zafar.

So playing with fire it is.

Jamilla looked at the tiny boats on the Mediterranean Sea far below them as the jet banked to head towards the Italian mainland. They had less than twenty minutes before the plane landed in Rome. After six days of diplomatic engagements in Italy they would be heading to Ireland and the Calhoun Stud.

She shuddered at the thought of the conversation she would need to have with Orla before they got there—to request the massive break in protocol she'd agreed with Dane to get him to wear an appropriate outfit so she could attend the ambassador's ball in Paris as his 'date'.

Jamilla's cheeks heated. She knew her employer. Orla wouldn't question the request, would totally sanction the break in protocol—she wasn't much of a stickler for that stuff anyway—and would be more than happy to lend Jamilla a ball gown she could have altered.

Because Orla totally trusted her. And would believe her when she said Dane had insisted she accompany him.

She glanced from her position by the jet's door to the seated area past the galley. Dane Jones was staring out of the window while talking on his phone to one of his management team in Manhattan. Her heartbeat bumped into her throat and the inappropriate thrill shot through her bloodstream again. The same inappropriate thrill which had made its presence felt when Dane had suggested their compromise.

The problem was, Jamilla wasn't sure if she trusted herself any more.

It was true, she hadn't suggested attending the ball with Dane, would never even have thought of it. And she suspected the reason he had suggested it was two-fold.

Firstly, he probably did prefer to have her with him—she'd noticed he seemed more conscientious about the role he was being asked to play when she was close by. He certainly seemed to have lost at least some of his animosity towards the Zafari monarchy since meeting some of his countrymen. And she was good at her job. She would be able to steer him discreetly if he needed it. And she would make a better wing woman if she were by his side.

But, much more disturbingly, she suspected he enjoyed provoking her and pushing her out of her comfort zone. No doubt it was a natural inclination for him, using his reckless charm to undermine a woman's defences… He had no real intention of seducing her. It was simply a game to him—a game being played for his own amusement to distract him from the rigours of representing Zafar.

The problem was it wasn't a game to her. Because she had so little experience of men—especially men like Dane Jones who oozed sexual confidence from every pore—she found it next to impossible to keep a lid on the inappropriate thrill when he showed her the slightest bit of attention. Which would be mortifying if it weren't so pathetic.

She sighed.

Thank goodness she had six days of state engagements in Italy and Ireland before they would travel to Paris and she would have to wear the gown. It would give her time to get the thrill under control. Hopefully.

She gripped the file folder she'd just retrieved from her briefcase. The folder she'd been intending to give to Dane when they boarded the plane four hours ago. But then he'd blindsided her with his Devil's bargain over the Paris ball and she'd chickened out.

How cowardly, and stupid, not to have given him the letters days ago. Why had she waited so long?

Because you want him to like you.

Dane ended the call and slipped his phone into his back pocket.

She steeled herself against the agonising pulse of regret and tightened her hold on the folder to walk towards his seat.

'Dane?' she asked, her breath backing up in her lungs, the inappropriate thrill sizzling when his gaze locked on hers. 'Could I speak to you for a minute?'

He frowned. 'Sure, as long as it's not another briefing about the schedule.'

She pushed out a strained laugh. 'No, it's…' She paused, sat in the seat opposite him and placed the folder on the table between them. A pulse of sadness played havoc with the zing of attraction. 'Saed found these with your father's personal effects. I thought you should have them back.' She pushed the faded folder across the table, regret sinking into her stomach like a stone. He would know for sure now, how callous his father had really been, and how indifferent he had been towards his second son. And he would surely hate her for enlightening him.

Dane frowned at the file of paperwork.

Weird. Why did Jamilla look so devastated?

It reminded him of the disturbing way she'd looked at him at the oasis after he'd let slip a little too much information about his childhood in Zafar.

'What's this?' he asked.

She didn't reply as he opened the file.

The frown deepened as he recognised the yellowing letter on top of the pile. The Manhattan postmark and the terrible handwriting threw him back to a time and a place he didn't want to return to.

He lifted the letter, saw all the others stacked underneath. So many others.

But then he noticed something about the envelope in his hand. It was still sealed.

Well… *Damn.*

'That son of a…' he hissed, then forced a wry laugh to his lips, ignoring the brutal tug in his chest—anger, pain, inadequacy—as the tiny flicker of hope he hadn't even realised was still there, after all this time, finally guttered and died.

So you got the letters, you bastard.

'I'm so sorry, Dane.'

He raised his gaze to find Jamilla watching him, compassion giving her amber eyes a soft glow.

The tug in his chest became a yank. 'What for?'

'For your father's appalling neglect. He was not a good King, this much I always knew, but he was also not a good man. Or a good father. Please do not be too sad.'

'Sad?' His lips quirked again; he couldn't help it. Was she actually serious? The sympathy and understanding in her expression was starting to unnerve him, reminding him of the kid he'd once been, scribbling those letters in the childish belief that his father would read them…and want to rescue him.

A guy who had never rescued anyone.

'Why would I be sad?' he asked, flicking the old letter back onto the pile with the disdain it deserved.

She seemed surprised. Good, he didn't need

her pity. That kid was long gone. And good riddance.

'Because...' she glanced at the letters '...he didn't answer the letters you wrote to him. You must have wondered why. After all those years.'

He shrugged. 'Not really.' Maybe he had once, but that kid had been a sap. 'She made me write them.'

'She?'

'My mom,' he said. Maybe it wasn't the whole truth, but it was true enough. 'She figured she'd be able to leverage more money out of him by having me beg him for it. She used up the divorce settlement pretty quick. But...' He looked back at the pile, thought of how Kitty Jones had made him take a break from running wild around the neighbourhood with his pals to write the letters once a month, without fail. It had been his mom's only rule—the only thing she'd insisted on.

She didn't care if he went to school, who he hung out with, where he was most nights or what he was doing, as long as he wasn't in her way. She'd told him often enough what a burden he was, how he'd ruined her figure and it had taken her years to get it back, how much he cost to feed and what a bastard his old man was. But once a month she would grab some stationery and insist he sit down and write those damn letters, the wheedling note in her voice one she only used when she wanted something.

'Make it sound good, baby. Tell him how we're struggling, how bad it looks when you're a Prince of Zafar and I can't even afford to feed you properly.'

He could still remember her standing over him in her boudoir, wearing one of her silk dressing robes, smelling of stale weed and her signature scent—a heavy rose perfume that went for two grand a pop—while puffing on one of the cigarettes she had shipped by the truckload from Paris, marching up and down like a drill sergeant. And the ever-diminishing balloon of hope as he'd written words he had finally figured out his father would never respond to.

Dumb, he thought. To think he'd once tried to kid himself the guy had never received them.

'I guess it backfired on her.' He shut the file, determined to shut out the feelings churning in his gut, and forced a brittle smile to his lips. 'It's actually kind of funny when you think about it. She went to all that trouble to make me write the damn things, but he never even bothered to read them. I guess he won that round in their war of attrition.' The war he'd been stuck in the middle of. Until he wasn't any more… Until his mom had told him…

He cut off the thought, shoved the collection of old letters towards her. 'Take them.'

She looked shocked by the command before she masked it. 'Um…okay.'

For a split second he imagined her as a kid. Winsome and cute. She'd probably been so well-behaved, so smart and hard-working, that dark hair in neat braids, those luminous eyes full of intelligence and purpose. He hated to think what she'd have made of him as a kid. He'd been a little bastard; even his mom hadn't been able to control him once he hit double digits—which was when she'd lost her temper and blurted out the truth, and he'd stopped writing those damn letters. And refused to believe in anyone any more.

Jamilla gathered up the file, still looking unsure. 'What do you want me to do with them?'

He shrugged. 'Throw them in the trash? Burn them? Hurl them off a cliff. I don't care. Do whatever you want with them. They don't mean anything to me. They never did.'

But as she walked away from him with the letters clasped to her bosom, he forced himself to ignore the stabbing pain where that dying flicker of hope had been, which was calling him a liar.

CHAPTER FIVE

'SO HOW DOES it feel to be properly acknowledged as a royal Prince of Zafar after being
thrown out of the kingdom as a boy by your father, King Abdullah?'

Dane squinted at the young female journalist in the front row. The bulbs flashed and the
cameras whirred around him as he ground his
teeth to stop himself from giving her a reaction
to the probing question. But inside the anger
built under his breastbone and all he could think
about were those damn letters Jamilla had tried
to return to him three days ago.

And how they confirmed what he already
knew. He shouldn't be here, posing as a prince.
When he was a fake. A phoney.

Jamilla tensed beside him on the dais set up
for this press conference at the exclusive six-
star hotel in Rome where the royal party was
based. A press conference he'd only agreed to
on the grounds he wouldn't have to talk about
this garbage.

'His Highness is not here to answer questions about his family's personal…' she began. But he held up his hand, cutting off her intervention. The question was out there now, no point in avoiding it or it would look as if he gave a damn—when he didn't.

'It feels great.' He realised his mistake as soon as he closed his mouth.

The press horde rose to their feet, firing out personal questions like piranhas who had just been chucked a hunk of fresh rib-eye.

'How do you feel about your father now?'

'Is it correct you returned to Zafar nine days ago for the first time in twenty-five years?'

'Why don't you use your father's name?'

'Are you planning to open any nightclubs in the desert?'

Most of the questions he couldn't hear, but the ones he did catch made fury twist and burn in his gut.

He had never courted publicity or used his royal credentials and this was why.

But then Jamilla leapt to her feet beside him, throwing her hands up in a quelling motion. 'I repeat, His Highness is not going to answer questions of a personal nature concerning him or his family,' she shouted above the horde, her voice firm, her stance furious on his behalf. 'He is here to represent the kingdom of Zafar on an important European trade tour. If you wish to ask him about his role here today, please do so.' She repeated the instruction in Italian then French and was finally able to lower her voice as the journalists started to sit back down and the barrage of questions was reduced to the odd shouted comment.

'Thank you,' she finally finished.

She pushed an errant strand of hair behind her ear, then brushed her fitted pants over her butt and planted it back on the seat. But the reaction that shot through him surprised him. Because it felt like more than just lust.

When was the last time anyone had protected him with such passion?

Disturbing emotion rippled beneath the heat.

This was their third day of engagements. And it was Jamilla Roussel's job to keep this press conference on the subject of the trade tour. She wasn't protecting him or defending his right to privacy, not really; she was simply making sure this tour did what it was supposed to do—promote Zafar's interests in Europe. And in this instance the country's new olive trade with Italy, the bumper olive harvest this year one of the big successes of Karim's agricultural revolution in the kingdom.

He forced himself to look away from her neck, the soft skin where her pulse pounded against her collarbone, the flush of exertion on her cheeks. He cast his gaze back over the piranhas and forced a smile to his lips which probably looked as brittle and unamused as he felt. Then he murmured, 'So, anyone got a question about olives?'

The ripple of laughter defused the tension in the room but did nothing for the tension in his gut as it occurred to him he had some kind of state banquet to handle after this—with Jamilla seated right next to him, no doubt wafting that sultry scent over him—before he could finally cut loose and shove the unpleasant emotions from his childhood back into the box marked 'ancient history'.

Great.

'Signorina Roussel, can I speak with you?'

Jamilla opened the door of her suite to find the man who was heading up Dane's security detail in Italy standing in the hallway. 'Hi, Enzo, what's the problem?' she said, anxiety squeezing her chest.

She'd left Dane an hour ago, outside the door to the hotel's luxury six-star penthouse suite. With three bedrooms, a giant terrace overlooking the Via Veneto and a full staff to cater to his every whim, Jamilla had hoped he would settle in for the night.

It had been an exhausting three days since they'd touched down at Rome-Fiumicino's International Airport. A string of formal introduc-

tions on their first day to the City's officials and
a host of national and European dignitaries had
been followed by a half-day trip to a factory in
Genoa. Dane had been the guest of honour at
a soccer match yesterday in Bari's magnificent
stadium—and today, after a tour of Florence,
she'd had to guide him through the hour-long
press conference back at the hotel.

Karim and Orla and their whirlwind romance
had captured a lot of media attention ever since
their engagement five years ago, but she'd hoped
the last-minute change of personalities would
have made the press hordes less voracious. No
such luck. Dane had always been something of
an enigma in the story of Zafar's royal family, so
his sudden appearance representing the monarchy had created a lot of speculation. She'd been
careful to brief the journalists beforehand on the
need to steer clear of any too personal questions.
But that hadn't stopped them.

He'd handled himself well, after she'd inter-
vened. But when they'd been whisked to a state
dinner afterwards she'd been all too aware of
his growing anger with the public scrutiny. And
she'd regretted even more their conversation on
the plane about the letters.

Why hadn't she simply kept them to herself?
Even though he had seemed uninterested in
them, unmoved, she'd sensed…something else
beneath the cynicism.

And the details he'd let slip about his mother had only disturbed her more.

Perhaps it was her projecting—probably—but she'd been only too happy when he'd insisted they leave the banquet as soon as all the toasts were done.

He'd been brusque and uncommunicative when they'd arrived back at the hotel. But she hadn't blamed him. Royal duties were much harder and more draining than they looked and, despite his heritage, Dane Jones had no experience of the work involved.

She was utterly exhausted now too—both mentally and physically—and they had another three full days of events before they left for Kildare on Monday morning. She'd already shrugged off her suit. She had a hot bath infused with her favourite bath salts waiting for her in the en suite bathroom. It was close to eleven and after spending the last twenty minutes finalising the schedule for tomorrow she was more than ready to spend the next twenty de-stressing before going to bed. She wanted to get up early tomorrow so she could get a run in and absorb at least some of the sights of the Eternal City— which she'd barely glimpsed from the back of their limo—before clocking back on at eight o'clock in preparation for their next official engagement at one.

Keeping a firm grip on her panic and exhaustion, she ushered Enzo into the room. If there was something Dane needed she was here to supply it.

'Um… I am very sorry, *signorina*, but His Highness is insisting on leaving the hotel without his security detail.'

'But he can't do that.' She blinked. 'It's for his own safety.'

And where was he even going? He'd looked almost as shattered as she felt twenty minutes ago.

'*Sì, signorina*, we explained this to him, but he insists. I thought it best to contact you. He has arranged to have a motorbike delivered; it will be impossible to protect him if he does not want us there.'

'Right…' She'd known keeping him corralled in the hotel would be a challenge. Reassuring him, convincing him not to put his own life in danger, was all part of her job. 'Okay, don't worry, I've got this.' She ushered Enzo out of the suite so she could get dressed again. 'I'll come straight up, just make sure he doesn't leave until I get there.'

'I will do my best, *signorina*,' Enzo murmured, sounding doubtful, which was not helping with her anxiety attack.

She got dressed in double-quick time, throwing on jeans and a T-shirt, a light sweater and a pair of boots. It wasn't how she wanted to present herself. Appearances were important and she'd already managed to put a huge dent in her professional relationship with Dane. But she didn't have time to reapply her make-up or have one of her power suits pressed.

She shot upstairs to the penthouse suite and rapped on the door.

Enzo answered with a mobile phone to his ear.

'Please tell me he's still here,' she gasped.

'He took the emergency stairs. I am coordinating a security detail to track him from the lobby...'

'Okay, great,' she said, cutting him off; maybe she could stop Dane if she caught up with him before he left the premises. 'You do that, and text me the details,' she said as she ran down the corridor, shoved open the fire exit door and raced down the concrete stairs—sending up a silent thank you that she'd opted for casual attire. She would have broken an ankle trying to pursue the man in four-inch heels.

Leaning over the metal railings, she spotted his wavy bronze hair two floors below. 'Dane, wait, can I speak to you?' she shouted.

His scowling face appeared briefly in the stairwell. 'I'm off the clock. Go back to bed, Jamilla.'

But you're never off the clock as the Zafari head of state.

She accelerated, flying down the steps. She finally caught up with him heading towards the basement level. So much for the security team waiting in the lobby.

'Please, Dane, you can't leave the building,' she said, struggling to catch her breath as she skidded to a stop in front of him, blocking his path into the hotel's underground garage. 'Not without your bodyguards.'

'Jamilla, get the hell out of my way.'

Large hands gripped her upper arms and he lifted her aside—with devastating ease.

But as he went to push open the heavy exit door she scrambled to wedge herself in front of him and pressed shaky palms to his chest.

The muscles flexed under the black T-shirt he wore with black jeans. And biker boots. Adrenaline shot through her, and into some unexpected parts of her body.

'Please, Dane, you can't go out alone. There are press out there. And possible threats.'

'What threats?' His brows drew into a sceptical frown. 'I've been stuck in here for three nights straight now.'

'Just…threats. You're a Prince of Zafar in Rome on an official visit!' she exclaimed, getting frantic now. Not least because of the adrenaline rush which seemed to have got lodged in her abdomen. The scent of him—clean laundry detergent and pine soap—and the flex of solid muscle beneath her palms did not help calm her racing heartbeat.

'Not right now I'm not,' he growled. 'I can handle myself just fine. And to hell with the press. If they want to chase me down, good luck to them.'

Grasping her arms again, he moved her to one side and shoved open the door. She had to ram her shoulder against the metal slab to stop it hitting her in the face.

A gleaming black motorcycle stood in a bay by the door. He fished a key out of the front pocket of his jeans.

Her mouth dropped open in horror as he swung a leg over the seat, fitted the key into the ignition, then lifted a helmet out of the saddlebag.

'You can't ride that—it's not safe!'

He simply stared at her for several long seconds, making the blush ignite her cheeks.

'Who made you my mom, Jamilla?' He clicked the key into the on position. 'Hell,' he muttered. 'Even my mom never gave this much of a damn!'

She didn't have time to contemplate the pang of tenderness at the snarled comment, when he kicked the ignition pedal and the engine roared to life.

She shot across the space, grasped his biceps

as he lifted the helmet. The bare skin seemed to sizzle against her fingertips.

'Don't go,' she pleaded, knowing she was concerned for more than just professional reasons. 'It's not safe. And I'll lose my job. I'm responsible for you, for your safety,' she added, getting more frantic by the moment.

She knew Karim and Orla would never blame her if something happened to Dane. But she would blame herself.

To her astonishment he paused. He stared at her, still brooding, that edge of fury she had sensed earlier, first when she'd shown him the letters, then at the press conference this afternoon, emanating off him. But then he thrust the helmet towards her. 'Put it on and climb aboard. If you're so worried you can come with me. But, either way, I'm outta here.'

'But I can't take your helmet!' she said, trying to shove it back.

He glared at her, his hands fixed to the handlebars as he revved the engine. 'Either put it on or stay here. Your choice.'

She slung the helmet on, clipped the strap and then hopped aboard the bike with more speed than skill. If she was with him, maybe she could alert Security to where they were. And talk some sense into him.

Once she was on board the rumble of the powerful engine sent shockwaves through her thighs. Her whole body was far too aware of his, with the memory of their torturous ride back from the oasis, as the bike kicked forward.

'Hold on,' he shouted.

She had less than a second to wrap her arms around his torso and cling on for dear life before they were shooting out of the parking garage and heading into the Roman night. And the shot of adrenaline wedged in her throat plummeted into her abdomen and hit critical mass.

Damn, the last thing he needed right now was Jamilla's toned curves—curves he'd been obsessing over way too much already—pressed against him. *Again.*

But as Dane wound down the tree-lined thoroughfare of the Via Veneto—putting his foot on the gas to zip past a lumbering delivery truck— the warm night breeze whipped his hair back and sent goosebumps rioting over his skin and he figured the additional torture was a small price to pay. To be free, at least for a little while, from the claustrophobic feeling of his past closing in around him.

A past he'd spent twenty-five years escaping from.

Damn his father and Zafar and all the pomp and circumstance he was going to have to endure for another two plus weeks yet to repay a debt to his brother. A debt his brother probably didn't even realise Dane owed.

Tonight he needed to be himself again. Not the public face of a monarchy that had spit him out as a kid. Tonight, he needed to be the guy who had worked his butt off to get away from that feeling of failure—and built his own business empire with no help whatsoever from the people who had made him a pawn in their disastrous marriage.

Veering off the main drag, he headed down a hill into a cobbled side street. He leant on the horn to scatter the tourists ambling in front of the bike like headless chickens.

He was forced to slow the bike to a crawl as they entered a piazza, inching past the stacked outdoor tables of pavement pizzerias, gelaterias and cafés filled now with tourists and locals alike, drinking strong coffee, sipping Limoncellos and Negronis or tucking into the luxury ice cream the area was famous for while soaking up the night-time energy to prepare for another long day in the sun. The pungent scent of tobacco smoke and frying garlic filled the air along with the exhaust fumes no doubt staining the laundry hanging above their heads, strung between the rows of neoclassical terraces.

He'd been to Rome before a bunch of times, knew his way around. But he could still remember Jamilla's wide-eyed wonder when they'd taken the limo past some of the city sights in the last few days, en route to their official engagements, and how she'd mentioned she'd never been to Europe before. He'd been kind of surprised, given her role in the royal household.

He made a spur-of–the-moment decision to take a right, heading through the labyrinth of alleyways towards the Piazza di Trevi. As they hit the square—still busy despite the clock being only a few minutes shy of midnight—her body jolted with surprise behind him.

Tourists milled around, mostly couples, but aboard the bike they had a clear view of the blue-green water lit from beneath, the triumphal arch and Corinthian columns of the Palazzo Poli providing an impressive backdrop for the famous fountain.

Water from the city's ancient source tumbled over marble. Neptune looked pretty pleased with himself in the centre of it all, lording it naked over the Tritons and what Dane figured were a couple of Vestal Virgins on either side of him.

He stopped the bike, a wry smile teasing his lips when Jamilla's arms loosened. He glanced over his shoulder and caught the same wide-eyed wonder in those striking amber depths he'd noticed a couple of times in the last few days. It sent a shiver through his body he didn't need and the smile died. How could she have that veneer of innocence when she was so smart and ambitious? Why did her artless enthusiasm seem like a direct challenge to his own jaded view of the world?

'It's so beautiful,' she murmured, like a kid in a candy store instead of the woman in a power suit and heels who'd handled the press so efficiently that afternoon. 'Thank you.'

Her gratitude poked at the tangle of emotion in his gut—the glimpse of the wonder-struck girl beneath the capable woman enchanting him in a way he didn't like.

He shrugged, trying to shake the feeling. 'No big deal; it was on my way.'

'Where are we going?'

'A place I opened on the Tiber a couple of years back. Thought I'd do an incognito spot check.'

'You own a nightclub in Italy?' she asked, the inquisitive frown reminding him of the woman and eliminating the girl, which only annoyed him more. Couldn't she forget about her job for one damn night?

'I own several.'

'But do you think that's wise—visiting it tonight when we have a full schedule of official engagements tomorrow? Also the press might be expecting you to…'

'Jamilla, if you want to hop off here and catch a cab back to the hotel to get a good night's sleep you can.' Why the hell had he invited her along anyway?

She shut her mouth and shook her head, the oversized helmet doing nothing to stop her direct gaze reminding him of the stubborn streak he'd seen a couple of times already.

'Then there are rules for tonight,' he said, deciding it was past time he set his own agenda here. This was his night, his escape and if she was going to tag along she needed to know that.

'What rules?' she asked, falling neatly into his trap.

'No talking about tomorrow's timetable or itinerary, or about your job or mine. If there's a problem with the press I'll handle it. And if you get tired I'll call a cab. But until that happens you're just a woman cutting loose and experiencing Rome for the first time. With me. So you do what I say, when I say it. You got that?'

'But…' Her eyes widened to saucer size and he could see what she was thinking as clear as day. That she couldn't trust him not to do something outrageous. Which, of course, just made him want to do something outrageous.

What was it about this woman that made him want to push her out of her comfort zone?

He'd been a fully-fledged bad boy as a kid. Running with the wrong crowd, dabbling in liquor and drugs, sleeping with women twice his age when he was still in his teens, getting on the wrong side of the juvenile courts a time or two—mostly just to infuriate his mom—and chucking away what little childhood he'd had left far too soon. But these days that tough, unruly kid was an astute and successful businessman who spent much more time working than hooking up, and had been clean and sober for over a decade. Why she should bring that reckless, impulsive boy back he had no idea, but he couldn't deny the adrenaline pumping through his system.

'But how do I know you won't ask me to do something…something dangerous?' she managed.

'You don't,' he said, playing Devil's advocate as the adrenaline rush he'd once been addicted to continued to power through his veins. 'You're just gonna have to trust me,' he added, knowing he couldn't even trust himself any more.

Tough.

She'd insisted on coming along for this ride, so she got to live with the consequences.

She chewed on her bottom lip, sending the visceral spurt of heat south.

'For once you're just gonna have to relax and enjoy the ride,' he added. 'You think you can manage that?'

He watched her debate the question, then figure out she didn't have much of a choice. It was his way or the highway and she was way too dedicated to her job to risk leaving him to his own devices. But then he saw excitement flicker in her eyes and his pulse jumped.

Sweet.

A part of her *wanted* to take a walk on the wild side with him. Even if she would never admit it to herself.

When she nodded he revved the bike's engine and felt her arms grip his waist, her full breasts plump up against his back. But this time, when the adrenaline rush hit hard, he smiled.

He finally had Jamilla Roussel where he wanted her. Time to stop letting her push his buttons and start pushing every one of hers.

CHAPTER SIX

Do not freak out. You're still doing your job. Sort of. You had to agree to his ultimatum. Sort of.

Jamilla repeated the mantra in her head, but it did nothing for the surge of exhilaration making her body hum and her heart bump against her ribs as she clung to the man in front of her and absorbed the incredible sights and sounds around her.

Up close, Rome was even more enchanting. But was that because of the wonderfully lived-in grandeur of the Baroque buildings that pressed in on them, the edgy energy of the nightlife spilling onto the city's streets even at midnight, the staggering beauty of the Trevi Fountain— a sight she'd imagined but never thought she'd actually see—and the other sights he'd already treated her to? Or was it the feel of Dane Jones's strong, powerful body, his clean musky smell, or the thought of spending a night out with a

man—a hot, exciting, charismatic and dangerous man like him—for the first time in her life?

*But you're not dating him; you're trying to
keep him safe. And out of trouble. Sort of.*

She swallowed down the twin tides of anxiety and excitement as the bike rumbled through
the narrow streets and out onto the banks of
the Tiber. He accelerated past the snarl of late-
night traffic, across a bridge and down a tree-
lined boulevard on the opposite bank. The wind
caught her hair beneath the helmet and brushed
her cheeks like a caress.

She tightened her grip, felt his abs ripple beneath her palms and buried her face against his
back. The clean scent of pine and bergamot only
added to the riot of sensation churning in her
abdomen.

Despite being so far outside her comfort zone
she was practically on Mars, she couldn't seem
to control the intoxicating adrenaline.

One night. Would it really be so wrong to let
go of the responsible, dedicated, diplomatic aide
for one night?

A part of her knew this had to be the romantic, irrational side of her nature she had inherited
from her mother—which she had ruthlessly controlled ever since she was a little girl, watching
her mother become distraught over a man who
had never loved her. Her mother had depended
on François Xavier Roussel, not just for love but

also for validation and self-respect. And he had denied all three —simply because he could. Jamilla didn't want to give any man that power, certainly not a man like Dane Jones, who was about as dependable as an unexploded bomb... But surely letting go for just one night didn't have to be bad? If she understood the risks.

Even so, as they arrived at a towering brick building on the waterfront—the neon sign announcing it as Jones Roma, the deep bass beat of a rap song pounding through the night air and the neoclassical arches on the upper floors pulsating with a rainbow of coloured lights—her heartbeat became ever more erratic.

Crowds of glamorous people stood outside as Dane parked the bike beside the river, waiting to gain entry to the exclusive venue. The women wore shimmering designer cocktail dresses and gravity-defying heels, their hairstyles and make-up like works of art. The men wore tailored suits and polished shoes, their hair perfectly styled too.

She climbed off the bike, her legs shaky, as Dane looped the bike's anchor chain around a tree, then took the helmet from her and stuffed it back in the saddlebag.

'Dane, I don't think we fit the dress code,' she said, staring down at her jeans and sweater combo. And imagining her face devoid of make-up and her now completely windblown hair.

Nerves tangled with the adrenaline and confusion, creating a volatile cocktail. Who was she kidding? She came from a desert kingdom which had only recently become culturally more liberal, following the end of King Abdullah's reign. They had nightclubs now in Zafar's capital city and youth culture was no longer suppressed, but even in university in Narabia she'd been dedicated to her studies and since then she'd been focused on her career.

She didn't do instant gratification or all-night clubbing. Especially when she had to be up first thing in the morning. But somehow—during the space of one wild ride—they'd leapt from her world into his, a world she had no clue how to negotiate.

Instead of giving her anxiety the attention it deserved, he simply sent her that criminally tempting smile. 'You quitting already, Jamilla?'

'It's not… I'm not…' Outrage surged through the nerves. 'This isn't about me quitting; it's just…' She lifted her arms. 'Look at me; I'm not even wearing any make-up. There's clearly a dress code.' She threw her hand out to indicate the people milling around across the street, ready to party the night away. 'And neither one of us is appropriately attired.'

He chuckled, the low rich sound somehow igniting the fire in her belly.

'Appropriately attired!' He laughed some

more, clearly at her expense. 'Give me a break. It's a club, Jamilla, not a diplomatic reception. You wear what you wanna wear. And no one's gonna be watching you, except me.'

He grasped her hand, and dodging a honking moped dragged her across the street. He strolled up to the main entrance as if he owned the place… Well, to be fair, he did.

The people standing in line outside shouted and gesticulated in outraged Italian, making Jamilla want to curl up and die on the spot. But Dane ignored the furore and spoke in surprisingly competent Italian to the doorman.

The bouncer released the rope instantly to usher them inside.

'You didn't tell them who you are, did you?' she asked. 'Because if he informs the press they'll…'

'Shut up, Jamilla,' he said over his shoulder.

She pursed her lips, trying not to panic even more. But as he dragged her down a shadowy hallway the panic receded, to be replaced by something that felt uncomfortably like awe.

The club's shadowy interior vibrated with sound, the noise and energy becoming louder as they got deeper into the darkness. The music began to throb in her bones as Dane cut through the crowd of hot gyrating bodies pulsing as one with the beat. The smell of sweat and abandon filled Jamilla's senses as the cramped corridor opened out into a huge cathedral-like space.

She craned her neck to take in the three tiers of pillared balconies that wrapped around the building. The majestic vaulted ceiling above them was open to the summer night, but did nothing to cool a dance floor alive with light and dry ice. People danced on platforms, in alcoves, arms high, bodies fluid; she could feel the shocked wonder squeeze her ribs as Dane spun her around, holding her steady as the crowd jostled. Someone pushed past them, nudging them so close together she could smell him—the salty aroma of sweat and the spicy, addictive scent of his cologne.

She stiffened, the last vestiges of that sensible woman clinging on for dear life. 'It's hot in here,' she shouted inanely, desperately trying to make small talk, to drag herself back onto solid ground.

'That's easily remedied,' he said, then grasped the hem of her sweater and pulled it up and over her head. He had tied it around her waist before she had a chance to gauge how exposed she felt in nothing more than a T-shirt and jeans—with none of her usual armour in place. She became brutally aware of the night air, which cooled her overheated skin but did nothing to stop the heat pulsing in her breasts as his hard chest brushed against the aching tips.

'Better?' he shouted, the mocking grin daring her to protest.

Clamping down on the moment of panic, she nodded, refusing to give him the satisfaction of seeing her freak out. And no longer able to deny the sensations coursing through her body.

He lifted her wrists, draped her arms over his broad shoulders, then placed his hands on her hips and tugged her into the lee of his body. She could feel him everywhere as he gyrated his hips, instinctively picking up the bass beat and letting it flow through his body and into hers. His palms caressed her waist, the anonymity of the darkness, the press of the crowd, the searing intimacy that cocooned them both terrifying and liberating in equal measure.

Holding onto his shoulders, she reached up on tiptoes. 'I can't dance; I don't know how,' she shouted into his ear, ashamed, embarrassed and yet still so alive. The yearning more intense now than it had ever been.

He pressed his thigh between her legs, ran callused palms under the hem of her T-shirt, sending sensation shimmering again over the bare skin of her back to join the electrical pulse in her nipples. He leaned down to press his lips to her ear. 'Then hold on tight.'

A part of her wanted to draw away. She'd never allowed herself to let go before, not entirely. But something about the night, the music, the wild feeling of abandon that had been intoxicating on the bike overwhelmed her now.

She moved with him, capturing the deep pulse of the music in the ebb and flow of her heartbeat—slow, seductive, unbearably arousing—fitting her curves into the hard line of his body, rejoicing when she felt his shudder of response.

She was playing with fire, she knew that, but just this once she refused to be careful and cautious, refused to extinguish the flames and instead let them sizzle and spark, flare and ignite.

This was just one night. One night free of responsibility, of propriety. He wasn't a prince and she wasn't a diplomatic aide. For the first time ever she was just a woman, with a devilishly attractive man. And all they were doing was dancing.

So instead of going with her first instinct—to run away from the shimmer of excitement and yearning, to scramble out of the devious well of desire he seemed intent on building around them—she threaded her fingernails into the short hair of his nape and let herself jump off the edge and into the abyss.

CHAPTER SEVEN

'Wow, I NEVER knew dancing could be so...fun!' Jamilla gripped the rail on the private balcony overlooking the Tiber as the night air cooled her heated skin, the buzz of excitement still pumping through her blood as she struggled to get her breath back.

How long had they been dancing? Hours it seemed as she noticed the purple light of dawn creeping across the dark blue sky that hovered over the cityscape.

But when she should have been panicked, concerned—after all, she had to be up and working in only a few more hours—all she felt was...energised.

She hadn't been familiar with any of the music but had adored every throb and flow of the beat, delighted in the guitar riffs which seemed to go on for ever, revelled in the siren song of voices, the cut and thrust of the wall of sound and scents cocooning them.

'You're a natural.'

She turned, the deep voice behind her rumbling through her torso and adding to the barrage of sensations still charging through her body. She'd never felt more alive, more powerful, more beautiful in her life.

It's an illusion, Milla, get a grip.

But even though her conscious mind was telling her to calm down, she couldn't control the intoxicating feeling of freedom and belonging still making her skin sparkle and zing.

Dane stood behind her, leaning against the wall. Sweat dripped down his temple but the rest of his face was cast into shadow. She could still feel the imprint of his body, the sensation of being forged in fire and sound.

Euphoria flooded through her, buoyed by the floaty feeling of exhaustion.

'You're a good teacher,' she managed, her voice rough with an emotion she didn't recognise but seemed powerless to stop.

He laughed, the sound wry but somehow lacking the cynical edge that had disconcerted her so much in the past. He stepped forward and those harsh, handsome features, that strong athletic build became gilded by moonlight. Her breathing, already ragged, thickened.

'You can't teach someone how to dance,' he said, the rueful tilt of his lips mesmerising her. Why had she never noticed before how beautiful his lips were, the sensual line only made more perfect by the rough stubble that had appeared during the night?

'Not that kind of dancing anyway,' he continued, the bergamot of his aftershave and the aroma of fresh sweat which had tantalised her on the dance floor combined with the muddy scent of river water and the potent perfume of the jasmine which clung to the wall behind him.

'In a club, after dark,' he added, his words dropping like bombs into the hum of exhaustion which had propelled them out onto the balcony after the final track had been played and the crowd began to disperse. 'It's all about gut instinct, letting go, feeling the beat. And not giving a damn what anyone else is thinking or doing.' He lifted a hand, as if in slow motion, and cupped her cheek.

Her breathing stopped abruptly, the feel of his palm in that moment—rough, sure, uninhibited—somehow more intimate than having his body pressed to hers for hours. Because now they were truly alone in the quiet dawn as the city woke up to a new day. The music had died, the stillness only interrupted by the hum of traffic and the thundering of her own heartbeat.

His thumb trailed across her lips and she opened them instinctively. She dragged in a desperate breath, unable to draw away from the purpose in that pure blue gaze or the devastat-

ing feel of his fingers sifting through her hair
as he cradled her head.

His movements were slow, deliberate, giving
her the chance to pull away. But she couldn't
obey the scream inside her own head telling her
to stop him, couldn't control the fierce tug of
yearning, the longing which had built to a crescendo as they'd danced.

'Who the hell knew you had it in you,' he
murmured, more to himself than her, 'to be so
wild?'

Her breath shuddered out and she flattened
shaky palms against his abdomen, felt the muscles jump and tense beneath his T-shirt. But instead of pushing him back, instead of telling
him no, her fingers fisted on the damp cotton
and she tilted her head back as his mouth—
so beautiful, so sensual, so demanding—found
hers at last.

She tastes as sweet and refreshing as she looks.
Better.

Dane thrust his tongue into the recesses of Jamilla's mouth, devouring the seductive taste of
her surrender. He wanted more—needed more.
His other hand rose to grip her head, the driving need exploding deep in his gut as her mouth
opened on a startled sob.

The need had been building for hours, every
time she moved against him, every time her

breasts brushed his chest, every time her hips rolled to bump against his thighs, every time her arms lifted and she threw her head back— her hair flowing, the ebony curls bouncing, cut loose from that damn ponytail hours ago—and raised her face to his.

She'd been stiff at first on the dance floor, scared, he guessed, to try something new and wholly inappropriate, but as soon as he had taken off her sweater and challenged her, something fundamental had shifted and changed. And then, as the night drew on, the crowd around them getting more rowdy, more in tune with the music, he'd watched her give herself over to the night. And to him... And he'd been mesmerised.

She'd always been stunning, but tonight she had become an enchantress, a queen, powerful and vulnerable at one and the same time, drawing him into her realm and making him want her.

Well, he was through watching, through waiting.

He lapped up her sighs, savouring the sultry taste of her passion, so potent, so intoxicating, so addictive. He angled her head to go deeper and feast on every last drop.

She shivered, her hands running under the hem of his T-shirt, touching the taut skin of his abs, making him shiver too.

Who was surrendering to whom here?

The last threads of his control stretched tight as need fired into his gut in fierce, furious waves, the throbbing weight in his pants painful. He walked her back until they hit the wall, cushioned in flowers. She trembled as he pressed the hard, heavy ridge into the soft cradle of her sex. She didn't resist, becoming more pliant, more delirious as he grasped her thigh, drew her leg up to hook it round his waist. He kept his lips on her neck as he pressed the painful ridge into the heart of her, rubbing the spot he knew would bring her some relief. Her head dropped back against the wall of flowers, releasing a puff of perfume from the blooms, the noise of traffic drowned out by her sobs of arousal.

He worked the spot through their clothing, nuzzling the sensitive skin under her chin, revelling in her response, his own breathing coming out in staggered gasps.

'Uh… Oh, God,' she whispered. 'I can't…'

'Shh… Just let it happen.' He kept rubbing while devouring her neck, feeling the frantic pulse of her heartbeat, ignoring his own pain to concentrate on her pleasure. He needed her to explode for him, needed her to go over, needed to make her surrender complete.

At last she tensed and her gasping cry of pleasure rang in his ears.

He dropped his forehead to hers, yanking himself back from that brutal edge, letting her body dissolve into his, the pain more than worth the stark joy of triumph.

He cradled her cheeks, looked into those beautiful amber eyes, dazed with afterglow. An afterglow he'd earned.

He tried to even his breathing, resisted the urge to yank down her jeans and panties, unzip himself and bury the brutal erection deep inside the tight warmth of her body so he could ease the pain too.

Not the time, not the place.

He pressed a kiss on her forehead, not trusting himself to take her mouth again—until they got back to the hotel room.

'That was even better than watching you dance,' he murmured, trying to find humour in the situation.

Didn't mean a thing that he'd just behaved like a lunatic, determined to get her off on the balcony of his own club. She'd got what she needed and so had he—or as much as he could get while they were in a public place bathed in the red glow of morning sunlight. Just a natural, elemental reaction to spending five solid hours dancing with her. No more, no less.

But even as he fought to drag himself back from the edge, shock shadowed her eyes and she drew her leg off his hip to break the intimate connection.

Her chin dropped, her gaze darting away, and

the vivid blush—that he had found so attractive
in the past—spread like wildfire, darkening her
skin, and only annoying him more.

'Hey.' He tucked a knuckle under her chin,
lifted her face, and saw panic and shame.
'What's wrong?'

She stiffened, then lifted her arm to scrape
her hair behind her ear. 'That...that shouldn't
have happened,' she said, her voice a whisper.
'I'm... I'm so ashamed.'

'Are you serious right now?' he demanded as
the turmoil in his gut turned to fury.

She finally looked him in the eye, and he
could see she was deadly serious. The fury became sharp and jagged.

'All I can do is apologise. Profusely.' She
glanced down and her cheeks ignited again,
probably because she could see the prominent
ridge in his pants. 'I behaved appallingly. And
unprofessionally.'

He ground his teeth together until his jaw
ached, controlling the urge to shout at her. To
tell her what he thought of her apology. But beneath it was that dumb kneejerk agony of rejection, of yearning, that reminded him of that
mixed-up kid who had searched for acceptance,
for affection, in sex. And never found it.

'You're not the only one out here,' he managed around the anger which was threatening
to choke him now. But which he couldn't let her

see. Because then she'd have got to him. And no woman got to him. Not any more. Because he wasn't that dumb reckless kid any more, the one who would take any scraps he was offered, any way he could get them. He didn't need that any more, not from anyone and certainly not from some uptight diplomatic aide who felt ashamed of having come apart in his arms.

Her gaze darted back to his. 'Yes, but I was the only one who…who…' She stuttered to a stop, obviously so mortified now by what they'd done, what she'd let him do, she couldn't even say it. So he said it for it.

'The only one who got off?' he asked.

Her throat flexed and he imagined her swallowing the bowling ball he could feel lodged in his own gut.

'Well…yes,' she said, the flush of embarrassment and regret making her cheeks glow.

'Don't get too cut up about it,' he said, forcing a cavalier smile to his lips that he didn't remotely feel. 'I'm a big boy. I'll survive.' He tried to unlock his jaw to make the smile more convincing. 'And you can shove the apology. Because those little sounds you made when you came were really hot. And I'll be sure to remember them next time you're busting my butt about the schedule,' he added, giving in to the desire to make her suffer as much as he was suffering.

If she thought she could just forget about this,

just pack it away into a neat little box marked 'big mistake' and go back to where they'd been, she had another thing coming. Because no way was that happening. He knew now who she was when she let her hair down, literally. When she let herself just be. He had smelt the sultry scent of her arousal, heard the sobs of her surrender, tasted those bee-stung lips. He'd done that, no one else. And now he knew she wanted him, the same way he wanted her.

And there was no way either one of them was going to be able to forget that.

'Please don't...' she began, but before she could complete the thought a glint of light from the street opposite caught his eye. He wrapped his arm around her waist and thrust her behind him.

'Damn...' He searched the embankment, above the line of traffic.

'What...?'

'Stay back,' he said, but he'd already seen the flash again as the photographer's telescopic lens caught the dawn light. He cursed loudly. 'We should head back,' he said, glad of the distraction.

'What did you see?'

'Nothing,' he said. Because what was the point in telling her? She was freaking out enough already.

And so was he.

CHAPTER EIGHT

JAMILLA WOKE SLOWLY, her mind fuzzy from sleep, her body aching from the rampant dream of...*him*.

She could hear a loud rhythmic buzzing in her head.

The memories from last night—the dangerous freedom of the dance floor, Dane's marauding lips, the scent of sweat and arousal and night-blooming jasmine, the fire exploding in her core—returned in a terrifying rush of sensation, propelling her out of that blank space between dreams and reality. She shot upright so fast she almost fell out of the deluxe king-size bed in her suite.

Oh, no.

She raked shaking fingers through her cloud of bed hair.

What had she done? It was almost as if Dane Jones had cast a spell on her with that glorious night ride through the sights and sounds of the city, the endless intimacy of the dance, the stunning dawn kiss when his hunger, his passion had driven her to heights she had never even known existed. But then it had all crashed and burned, the seductive night giving way to the stark reality of dawn.

Except this isn't his fault—it's yours.

The shame descended, like a black cloud covering the sun.

She'd crossed so far over the invisible line between them—a line she was fairly sure she would never be able to uncross.

They'd returned from the club in silence. The ride through the dawn, past the Trevi Fountain, round the Spanish Steps, along the Via Veneto should have been enchanting, but as she'd sheltered behind him on the motorbike, her cheek pressed against the tensed muscles of his spine, all she could see was the fury on his face after their kiss.

She'd angered him, she could see that—with her shame, her regret—because she suspected he didn't understand propriety, appropriate behaviour, didn't care about the strictures by which she had always lived her life. That his devil-may-care pursuit of pleasure—*her* pleasure—only made him more intoxicating, more mesmerising, just made the position she'd put herself in now all the more dangerous.

The loud buzzing began again and she jumped. Her phone was ringing.

Fumbling for it on the nightstand, she glanced at the screen. Orla was calling her, and it was already half past eleven in the morning!

She blinked at the endless string of missed call alerts from the different media contacts she had been dealing with for weeks.

But the panic about the job ahead of her this morning didn't come, because the job was the least of her worries now.

Guilt swelled in her chest. She let the phone ring a few more times, gathering herself for the awkward conversation she was going to be forced to have with a woman she had always respected. A woman who she considered a friend. A woman who had trusted her. A woman she had failed miserably last night. Just the way she'd failed the monarchy, the country and the mission that Karim and Orla had assigned her.

Just as she had failed herself.

She sucked in a tight breath round the ache in her chest. Lifting the phone, she clicked the answer button with trembling fingers.

'Jamilla, are you okay?' Orla jumped in before she could say anything. She sounded concerned, even a little frantic. The guilt grew into a boulder under Jamilla's breastbone.

'Yes. I'm so sorry, I overslept.'

Orla gave a small laugh—both relieved and rueful. 'Well, I suppose that's to be expected.'

'It is?' Jamilla asked, confused now as well as heartsick.

'Yes, listen, Jamilla. I just called to check you're okay and to let you know that Dane texted Karim early this morning. And Karim and I have had a long conference call with Jed and Alicia,' she continued, mentioning their press secretary Jed Allingham and Alicia Van Dusen, the top media consultant who Jamilla had been liaising with on the tour. 'To find the best way forward before the news broke.'

News? What news?

'We all think we should cancel the rest of the week's engagements in Italy. Jed feels the press intrusion will be brutal, so it makes sense for you and Dane to fly to County Kildare today so you can take the next five days to regroup while we figure out how best to play this. The tour isn't as important as both of you.'

Dane had texted the King? This morning? *When* this morning?

Shock came first, swiftly followed by nausea. Had he told Karim about what they'd done?

'I just wanted to talk to you, Jamilla, to make absolutely sure you're really okay.' Orla's voice dropped, concern etched in every single syllable.

Jamilla's mortification increased ten-fold. Orla was being so considerate, so thoughtful, and she didn't deserve it. But another part of her was still hopelessly wary and confused. Why had Dane texted Karim? Had he boasted about what had happened? Had the whole night been a trap to destroy her credibility?

The thought horrified her.

He'd been angry with her last night, angry with her reaction to his kiss, and she still didn't really understand why. But she would never have guessed he was the kind of man to brag about his conquests. Or to deliberately try to destroy her reputation. But how much did she really know about him?

The sick feeling of dread became lodged in her gut.

'The young woman on that balcony seemed so different from the woman I know you to be,' Orla added. Jamilla's pulse rate hit the stratosphere. How did Orla know so much? 'But I just want you to know that doesn't have to be a bad thing. And you'll be finding no judgement here.'

'Dane told Karim about last night?' The words were propelled out of her mouth on a breath of stunned horror.

He had told the King about her kissing him like a wild woman, giving herself up to the moment? Mortification engulfed her.

Was she still asleep? Still dreaming? Because this was a nightmare.

'Oh, Jamilla, I'm so sorry,' Orla said, her voice regretful now as well as full of compassion. 'I'm guessing you haven't seen today's headlines. Dane didn't give us any details, all the text said was that there might be a problem as he'd seen a photographer last night, taking pictures of the two of you. Karim hasn't managed to get in touch with him since. Anyway, we tried through several channels to have the photos contained but unfortunately they're all over the press and the internet.'

'*Ph...photos?* Photos of what?' She had to slap her hand over her mouth, the nausea barrelling up her throat. But behind it was also a strange sense of relief that Dane hadn't tried to destroy her. That in his own blunt way he had been trying to protect her.

'Of you and Dane last night, on the balcony of his club in Rome,' Orla said calmly. But not nearly calmly enough to stop Jamilla's whole body shaking. 'Kissing each other as if your lives depended on it.'

A swearword Jamilla had never spoken in her entire life shot out of her mouth.

'There are photos of us? Together? Kissing?' she hissed, worn out with the barrage of emotions after so little sleep. She couldn't seem to put any of it into perspective any more. 'In the media?' she said, trying to make it all seem real when it still felt like a terrible dream.

Even if Dane had tried to protect her, her reckless behaviour, her monumental lack of judgement was now out there, displayed for all the world to see.

'I'm afraid so. I'm sorry, Jamilla. I know what a private person you are. And this is beyond intrusive. I feel absolutely terrible for you both, that you should be put in this position. And especially as a result of your work for Zafar—and Karim and me.'

Jamilla registered the compassion still thickening Orla's voice, and the regret. But it made no sense. Why should Orla or Karim feel responsible when she was the one who had destroyed everything? Panic rose up her throat now to join forces with the nausea.

'I will resign, effective immediately, of course,' she managed to get out as the weight in her stomach reached catastrophic proportions.

'Resign?' Orla sounded genuinely shocked. 'Jamilla, don't be silly. Why should you resign? It's not your fault some sneaky gobshite climbed up a tree and took pictures of you both in a private moment to sell to the highest bidder.'

'Yes, but…'

I was the one who kissed Dane Jones as if my life depended on it. Because in that moment it felt as if it did.

'But nothing,' Orla interrupted, cutting off the words Jamilla was trying to get up the guts to actually enunciate. 'I'll not have you feeling guilty for the behaviour of the tabloid press. That man had no right to…'

'But I did kiss him,' she managed to get out, the guilt only made worse somehow by Orla's unwavering support. 'I disgraced myself and my role as a representative of the Zafari monarchy. I threw myself at him, I lost control and behaved like a…a…' She stuttered to a stop. She couldn't even say the word.

'Jamilla, it was just a kiss,' Orla said so gently Jamilla's eyes stung.

'It was more than a kiss,' Jamilla said as she scrubbed away the tear that leaked out, the tightness in her chest making it hard to breathe.

Orla gave a soft laugh. 'Well, yes, it looked like a bit more than a kiss. But seriously, Milla,' she added, using the nickname Jamilla had always felt cemented their friendship. 'It was after hours. You're entitled to a private life. And Dane kissed you right back, and I'll be betting he initiated it. Because I'm guessing the man has a mite more experience in these matters than you do. And he's also a total ride,' she added, using the Irish vernacular for hot. 'Although don't tell Karim I said that—he's a bit sensitive about me noticing how hot his brother is, even if it is in a purely observational capacity.'

Was Orla joking now? Jamilla sniffed loudly, trying to hold onto the sobs that were starting to crush her ribs and see the funny side, although she was finding it hard to locate anything at all amusing about the whole situation.

'But I've ruined everything,' she said, giving in to misery again. 'You're going to have to cancel the tour. Can't you see I can't be trusted any more? To do my job. To make sensible decisions. I've ruined everything.'

'Jamilla, no, you haven't. We're not suggesting cancelling the tour, just the rest of the engagements in Italy so the story has a chance to calm down,' Orla said, putting on the firm voice she used with her young son whenever he was tired or cranky. 'You've always set such a high standard for decorum. But you're human. And nobody would even know this had happened if it wasn't for that horrible paparazzo.'

'But I'd know,' Jamilla said. And Dane knew.

'Well, yes, you would. And I think we should definitely have a girl talk once you're here to discuss what's actually going on with my brother-in-law. But that's a personal matter. When it comes to the professional aspects of your role, I wanted you to know that Karim and I still trust you implicitly to do the job you've been asked to do. The real question is do you want to continue working so closely alongside Dane? Now that there appears to be a personal aspect to your relationship with him—and, unfortunately, thanks to that bastard photographer, the press will no doubt be focusing on it during the rest of the tour—we'd totally understand if you would prefer to be reassigned.' Orla sighed. 'I'll admit I don't know Dane that well; he's something of an enigma. Karim acknowledges that he's always had, shall we say, an *effect* on women. Karim doesn't believe he's an untrustworthy person or that he would ever exploit a woman, but they're brothers. I don't want Dane taking advantage of you, however inadvertently...' She added carefully, 'Or for you to feel pressured in any way.'

The memory of the devastating orgasm, the way she'd let go without a thought to the consequences and the argument between them that had followed chose that precise moment to flow through her head in vivid Technicolor. Shame washed over her all over again.

But he didn't take advantage of me. If anything, I took advantage of him.

Dane hadn't wanted her to go with him. He'd only agreed to take her along last night because she'd insisted. And while she'd been telling herself it was so she could keep an eye on him, make sure he didn't go AWOL, she could see now the reality had been different. She'd somehow persuaded herself she was doing her job, when her motivations hadn't been nearly that simple. Or altruistic. She'd seen the frustration on his face, the need to escape, and a part of her had wanted to soothe him, like some wild beast who needed to be tamed. Which just made it all the more humiliating—and ironic—that as soon as she'd climbed aboard his bike the opposite had happened.

He'd tempted her wild side out of hiding, but it really hadn't taken that much of an effort. Because that wild side had always been there, just waiting to burst free. And what made it even worse was that she could see clearly now, she had feelings for him—perhaps triggered by the conversation they'd had about his father's letters, perhaps before that, when he'd spoken about Zafar at the oasis. She'd realised how hard it was for him to take on the role he'd committed to, and secretly she'd admired that. Not only that, but she'd somehow convinced herself they had a connection, because of her difficult relationship with her own father.

Maybe François Xavier Roussel had never been as callous as King Abdullah, but he had abandoned her mother without a backward glance, and ultimately abandoned her too. Somehow, subconsciously she'd been looking for his approval ever since. So much so that she had completely repressed her natural urges, eventually becoming like a pressure cooker, ready to blow at the first sign of temptation. Perhaps she needed to address that reaction because it had surely intensified her attraction to a man she barely knew.

'I wasn't pressured to do anything I didn't

want to do,' she managed in answer to Orla's last question.

She'd made choices, bad choices maybe, but they had been her choices. Not Dane's.

'Okay, well, that's good.' Orla breathed out as if she'd been holding her breath, and Jamilla felt a wave of love for her employer. Her friend. 'And so how do you feel about continuing with the tour, as Dane's diplomatic advisor? Karim said Dane made it clear in his text he didn't have a problem with continuing. Which suggests you're doing a great job with putting him at his ease in the role.' She laughed again. 'In a professional capacity, of course.' Her voice sobered. 'But if you want to return to Zafar, we can assign someone else. No questions asked.'

But I don't want to leave him. He needs me.

The thought came out of left field. She swallowed, gripping the phone, and stared out of the large mullioned windows of the suite. She pulled her legs up in the bed to hug her knees one-handed as she tried to subdue the emotion in her chest.

A part of her knew she ought to accept Orla's offer. Spending time with Dane was dangerous in so many ways. She had become emotionally invested in him in more ways than one.

But another part of her didn't want to give up. However misguided her emotions, however dangerous the desire that had blindsided her, she needed to find a way past it.

Because she could see now her fall from grace last night wasn't just about Dane. It was also rooted in that confused, desperately obedient little girl who had tried so hard to make her father care for her and had never understood why he had chosen to live in France with the children he'd had with his mistress instead of her and her mother.

Dane had given her the male attention she'd always craved for one wild night. And she'd lapped it up. She had to get that into perspective.

'I don't want to be reassigned,' she said. 'I'd like to continue with the tour. And see it through.' She couldn't quit. She'd started this job and she needed to finish it, if for no other reason than to prove to herself she could.

'Okay, grand. I hoped you'd say that,' Orla said, sounding a lot more confident than Jamilla felt.

The confidence will come, if you keep the professional distance with Dane you lost so catastrophically last night.

But as they finished the call and spoke of next steps, including the arrangements for Dane and her to travel to Ireland that afternoon, Jamilla could feel the pressure in her chest increasing at the thought of the weeks ahead, working closely with Dane while trying to keep her wayward emotions, and the reckless desire, under wraps.

Once she'd ended her conversation with Orla she received a call from Enzo, alerting her to the fact the press had been camping out at the hotel, ready to waylay her and Dane.

She switched off her phone and headed for the shower. She turned the dial from hot to frigid in an attempt to wake up and wash away the last of the panic and confusion still working its way through her system.

Strangely, though, as her tired body responded to the needle-sharp spray, the thought of reorganising the rest of the tour and running the press gauntlet didn't feel anywhere near as daunting as facing Dane again.

CHAPTER NINE

'WHERE THE HELL have you been, Dane?' Karim shouted over the helicopter noise as Dane jumped from the large black Puma onto the field in County Kildare.

The King of Zafar looked remarkably at home on the back pasture of the Calhoun stud farm wearing worn jeans and a T-shirt and with his arms full of his toddler son, Hasan. But the little boy's wide smile of welcome when he spotted Dane was in direct counterpoint to his father's accusatory frown.

Figures.

'We were expecting you here four days ago,' Karim added as the chopper Dane had co-piloted from the rooftop of his London club for the journey to Ireland finally powered down enough to make speech less of an effort.

'Good to see you too, bro,' Dane murmured, keeping the forced couldn't-give-a-damn smile he'd been working on for four days firmly in place. Ever since his night in Rome with Jamilla…and that kiss.

The kiss he hadn't been able to forget, no matter how hard he'd tried. And he'd tried. A lot.

She'd been silent, they both had, on the ride back to the hotel that night. He'd alerted Karim to the possibility of the photos, then crashed. The next day he'd caught the headlines and been mad as hell about them. But after ducking out the back of the hotel and taking a ride through Rome to the Colosseum to clear his head, he'd been ready to confront Jamilla about what had happened and what to do next.

The tabloid headlines were bad news, sure. But, the way he saw it, they weren't anywhere near as big a problem as the chemistry they'd ignited on the balcony of his club. Or the emotions churning in his gut at the way she'd freaked out about it.

But when he'd arrived at her suite that afternoon he'd been told she'd already left for Kildare. Apparently, she'd arranged to have him travel separately to Ireland, to avoid the paparazzi getting another shot of them both together and pouring more fuel on the media bonfire before their time out. Or at least that was what the young assistant she'd had waiting for him in his suite had told him. Which sounded smart and reasonable.

He wasn't buying it for a second.

The truth was, she hadn't wanted to see him in the flesh again until she got herself back under control, hadn't wanted to deal with the fallout from that kiss and the sweet sexy climax he'd treated her to. She was running scared. Of him, of the heat between them, just as much as those tabloid headlines. She'd probably figured that by engineering the next meeting between them in Kildare—with Karim and Orla and little Hasan acting as chaperones—he'd be happy to just pretend it had never happened.

Yeah, well, he'd tried that, deciding to give her some space until he was good and ready to see her again too. So, instead of taking the Zafari royal jet which was fuelled and waiting at Rome-Fiumicino, he'd packed a bag, switched off his phone and headed off on the bike to wind his way up through Florence, Genoa, Milan, then across the Alps into France to clear his head. He'd finally switched on his phone again when he'd got to London to pick up his company chopper to County Kildare.

There had been a ton of messages from Karim, the press secretary, his own PA in Manhattan—who had probably been hounded by his brother's staff to find out where the hell he was. The only person who hadn't messaged him in those four days was the woman who the last time he'd seen her had been flushed and wary and showing the first signs of beard burn from his kiss.

I rest my case.

He swept his hair back and ignored his brother to grin at his nephew. 'Hey there, little buddy,' he said, giving the kid a poke in the stomach which elicited the expected belly laugh.

'Unca Dane!' the little boy shouted and stretched out chubby arms.

He scooped Hasan out of his father's arms, ignoring the emotion that hit him at the realisation that his nephew had remembered him. The boy began chattering to him in that language only toddlers understood—providing a handy distraction from Karim's questioning frown—as they headed towards the house. But, weirdly, when he was forced to put the boy down so the kid's nanny could take him in to have his supper, the ripple of emotion turned into a pang.

He wasn't a family guy—he had decided years ago he never wanted to be a father himself. The fallout from his night with Jamilla—and the emotion wedged in his gut at the thought of seeing her again, and finally having it out with her, whatever the hell *it* was—had obviously done an even bigger number on him than he thought.

Something he liked even less than the snarky question his brother shot at him once the boy and his nanny were out of earshot.

'Why didn't you answer any of my messages?'

Karim demanded. 'And where the hell *have* you been? Because that was a genuine question, *bro*,' he added, stressing the word bro in that sarcastic, self-righteous way he had that had always got on Dane's nerves.

He owed his brother a lot, for letting him tag along during his early years in the kingdom, when his brother had visited in the summer— and for keeping tabs on him as a teenager during his exile in Manhattan, when no one else had given a damn about him. Certainly not his mother or their father. But that didn't give Karim the right to boss him about.

'I didn't answer the messages because I switched off my phone,' he replied, struggling to keep his temper under control. 'And where I was is none of your damn business.'

'Well, that was remarkably irresponsible, even for you,' Karim shot straight back. 'And actually it is my business. If you recall, we have a royal trade tour which has just had to be completely rescheduled because you chose to play fast and loose with our chief diplomatic aide.'

His temper exploded like a bomb at Karim's accusation. Words he'd been expecting ever since he'd contacted Karim to give him a heads-up about the photographer. But right beneath the anger was the sting of guilt, thanks to an image that had been bugging him ever since that night. The shadow of shame and humiliation in Jamilla's wide amber eyes, and the reddening mark on the soft skin of her chin.

He shoved his brother back against the garden wall, his arm coming up instinctively to press against Karim's throat. 'You son of a...' he hissed, the forced smile forgotten as he let the anger boil over to cover the sharp sting of guilt. 'I'm not a kid any more, screwing anything that moves.'

And so desperate for affection I figured I could find it in indiscriminate sex.

He swallowed down the humiliating thought, let the fury build to disguise the hole in his gut he thought he'd sealed up a long time ago. 'I kissed her, she kissed me. Got it? She's a grown woman who gets to make her own decisions. I didn't force her. And it's not my fault some sneak took a photo and decided to splash it all over the front pages of the gossip mags. The French leg doesn't start till tomorrow and I'm here now, aren't I?'

'Dane, chill out,' Karim murmured, lifting his palms in a universal sign of surrender, his brother's expression registering shock not judgement. 'I apologise; that was out of order.'

Dane dropped his arm, stepped back, feeling shaky now and tense, and embarrassed by the outburst and the fury still pitching and rolling in his stomach.

'I know you didn't force her,' Karim continued, still staring at him as if he had lost his mind.

Dane raked his fingers through his hair. Hell, maybe he had.

'Jamilla has told us as much, but even if she hadn't, I know that's not the kind of man you are.' Karim placed a hand on his shoulder, squeezed.

Dane shrugged, humiliated now, not just by his outburst but by the knowledge of how much Karim's confidence in him still meant.

Karim had always believed in him, even when he didn't deserve it. That was why his brother had loaned him the money to buy his first stake. He'd paid that investment back with interest a long time ago. So why the hell should he think he'd failed him somehow? Or still care so much about what he thought of him?

'All right, thanks, apology accepted,' he murmured, feeling surly now as well as unbearably tense. 'I said I'd continue with the tour and I will,' he added tightly. 'I just needed some time to clear my head. Okay?'

'Of course,' Karim replied.

Dane looked away, not quite able to meet his brother's searching gaze. He didn't want to see the questions there—questions he couldn't even answer himself.

He'd overreacted to Karim's offhand comment, that much was obvious. And Karim was probably wondering why.

Yeah...good luck with that one, bro.

As he struggled to calm his breathing and douse the last sparks of his temper, his gaze landed on the majestic eight-bedroom Georgian manor house where Karim and his family had been living for the last few months. And where Jamilla had been too for the last four days—no doubt rearranging the tour dates and waiting for the world's press to move on.

The collection of brightly coloured toys discarded on the front lawn alongside a small slide and a little orange pedal car, the lovingly tended vines that clung to the red bricks, currently spotted with spring blooms, the sparkling clean windows which looked out over the lush green fields and the racing stables and the gallops beyond all seemed to mock him now as unfamiliar and inexplicable emotions still refused to settle in his gut.

Karim had restored the Calhoun family's ancestral mansion to its former glory for his wife after their marriage five years ago. His brother's family used the place on and off during the racing season when Orla was managing the stud— or awaiting the birth of their kids.

He'd visited them here several times in the past. Mostly as a compromise, because he'd refused to accept any of the invitations they'd sent him to visit them in Zafar. He'd never had a problem with being here, until now.

But this wasn't just a house any more, however grand, it was a home, he realised. And yet another place where he would never truly belong.

Why did that bother him, though, when it never had in the past?

Then he spotted two figures walking across the fields from the stable yard, chatting. He recognised his sister-in-law from her slow, uncomfortable gait and the silhouette of her rather impressive belly. The other woman, her dark hair falling in loose waves past her shoulders, her taller, slimmer figure dressed in a white blouse and dark jeans, should have been harder to recognise from this distance.

Except she wasn't. Because his body reacted instantly to that graceful physique, those slender curves.

Jamilla.

Her name whispered across his consciousness as all his senses shot straight back into the danger zone.

So that answered one question, at least.

Taking a four-day solo bike tour through the back roads of Italy and France, camping out and taking full advantage of the freedom of the road, hadn't controlled the hunger or the impact of that night one little bit—if anything, it had made it worse.

Her head rose, almost as if she'd sensed him standing there watching her, and she stopped dead.

All of a sudden her movements looked a lot less graceful, a lot less relaxed. The emotions in his guts fired up to go with the heady kick to his senses. Her stance reminded him of a young doe he'd caught in his truck's headlamps one night while heading to his farm in Upstate New York. He'd slammed on the brakes to avoid hitting the beautiful creature and she'd bounded back into the forest before he'd had a chance to really appreciate her.

He kept his gaze locked on the beautiful creature in front of him this time as he set off across the fields towards her. He could see as he got closer that her desire to bolt was even stronger than the young doe's.

But she didn't move. She stood her ground and waited for him to reach her and Orla, her arms wrapped around her midriff, though, as if bracing herself for the inevitable confrontation.

Smart woman. Because there's no way I'm letting you run away from me—or this thing between us—again.

This woman had got under his skin in a way no other woman ever had. And he still didn't know why exactly. The heady need swelled in his groin at the flicker of awareness in her eyes as he approached.

And the confidence which had eluded him for days returned in a rush.

Maybe the answer to their problem wasn't all that complicated after all. Perhaps it was simply time they both stopped running from the inevitable.

'So I see Dane finally turned up,' Orla murmured beside Jamilla.

But Jamilla could hardly hear her friend's comment above the thundering in her ears.

He looked…magnificent, his bronze hair lightened by the sun, his skin tanned a darker brown. The white T-shirt showed off the defined contours of his pectoral muscles, while the frown on his face and the purposeful stride suggested he had a lot to talk about.

Her reprieve was over.

She'd been preparing for this confrontation for four days. She'd gone through every possible permutation of how she was going to tell him—succinctly and without any flicker of the emotion currently turning her insides to mush—that they needed to put the events of that night behind them, go back to how they had been before she'd climbed aboard his bike and become a wild woman. She couldn't afford to lose herself again, and she needed his help to ensure the rest of the tour went off without a hitch. That kiss had been a mistake—a massive mistake that neither one of them wanted to repeat, surely.

But what had all seemed so simple, so obvious—while she'd stared at the ceiling above her bed late at night or spent hours deflecting the endless press enquiries with well-rehearsed platitudes about Rome's eternal beauty and its ability to make anyone lose their mind, or took on the titanic task of rearranging the tour commitments so she would be spending as little time as possible in Dane's company—suddenly seemed a lot less simple or obvious.

'He looks like he's got rather a lot to say to you,' Orla added while he was still out of earshot. 'Do you need me to stay?'

'No,' Jamilla said as forcefully as she could manage with the panic starting to choke her.

She'd been enough of a coward already. If she hadn't taken the opportunity to leave Rome ahead of him she could have had this situation done and dusted by now, instead of having it turn into a lump of radioactive waste in her stomach over four restless days and sleepless nights while he'd done his disappearing act. Getting their working relationship back on track was her only priority. And that meant standing her ground and not freaking out.

Reaching them at last, Dane nodded at his sister-in-law but his gaze barely left Jamilla's.

'Hey, Orla, you're looking...' a smile curved his lips which didn't quite make it to his eyes '...enormous.'

Orla let out a half laugh, doing her best to defuse the tension. 'Gee, thanks, bro,' she muttered. 'Now I feel like even more of an elephant.'

He leaned past Jamilla and gave his sister-in-law a brotherly peck on the cheek. 'If it's any consolation, the elephant look suits you, sis.'

'You rat,' she said, giving him a slap on the arm, but then she laughed, the amusement more genuine this time. The pretty flush of pleasure on her face at Dane's compliment made Jamilla realise this man could charm any woman if he put his mind to it.

But the reckless twinkle in his blue eyes hardened to steel as his gaze landed back on her.

'Hey, Orla,' he said, never breaking eye contact with Jamilla. 'How about you leave Jamilla and me alone for a minute? We've got a lot to discuss.'

Jamilla's blush intensified at the direct, assessing look and the heat in it he was making no attempt to hide.

She'd told Orla all about the kiss, what had led up to it and how ashamed she was of the way she'd behaved. Orla, being Orla, had continued to shrug off all Jamilla's guilt and angst and *mea culpas*. Orla had also made it clear that whatever Jamilla wanted to do about Dane, and that kiss, going forward, she and Karim would not judge her. Orla had even told Jamilla quite a lot about her own courtship with Dane's brother, which had turned out to be not nearly as straightforward or picture perfect as Jamilla had always assumed. The news that Orla had effectively been 'contracted' as Karim's fiancée before they'd fallen in love for real had been nothing short of mind-blowing.

But, despite the confidences Orla had shared, Jamilla didn't believe her situation with Dane was remotely similar. Orla hadn't been in a working relationship with Karim, not really, despite that contract. And it was obvious the two of them were made for each other. Unlike herself and Dane.

Jamilla had been deeply touched by Orla's support. But she hadn't been able to get up the guts to tell her friend she wasn't quite as worldly wise or pragmatic when it came to intimate relationships as Orla had clearly assumed. And that she had absolutely no prior experience of having been—quite literally—swept off her feet by her desire for a man.

A desire that had burned every night since and was burning now. Along with her indignation at Dane's high-handed decision to have this conversation as soon as he arrived.

I mean, seriously, could he have made this

situation any more inappropriate with his de-mand for privacy?

'I can leave you guys alone,' Orla said. 'If that's okay with Jamilla?' she added, sending Jamilla a pointed look that clearly stated: *Whatever you want to do now, you have my support.*

Gratitude came first, followed by the twist of cowardice.

If only she could say, *No, I don't want to have this conversation. It's too much, he's too much. Just being this close to him makes me want to do stupid things again.*

But she banked the spurt of panic, attempted to swallow it whole, along with a wave of mortification.

I'm not afraid of him or how he makes me feel, she added to herself, and tried to make herself believe it.

The nerves in her belly became more volatile and persistent. But she forced herself not to leap at the lifeline Orla offered. This was her mess to clean up. No one else's.

'Yes, it's fine, Orla,' she said.

Orla gave her and Dane one last look, then nodded slowly. 'Okay, I should go and help get Hasan fed and in bed,' she said. 'We'll see you both for dinner at eight?'

'Great, thanks,' Dane said, still not taking his eyes from Jamilla's flaming face.

And then Orla was gone. And it was just the two of them.

Jamilla sucked in an unsteady breath when he didn't say anything, just continued to stare at her, the temper still sparking in his eyes she'd noticed the last time she'd seen him. When he'd bid her a perfunctory goodbye in the hotel's garage. Before she'd raced up to her suite, and tried without success to dismiss the buzz on her lips, the sting on her cheeks, the deep throbbing ache at her core.

She struggled to recall the speech she'd been working on for four days. The forthright, apologetic speech about decorum and mistakes and professionalism and appropriate behaviour. But she couldn't remember a single word of it.

And something else entirely burst past her lips. 'Where have you been? The Paris ball is six days away. We're travelling tomorrow and I haven't had a chance to brief you on the media strategy we've worked out. *Or* the changes to the itinerary.'

He tilted his head to one side, that heated gaze narrowing on her flushed face. His temper flared like a firecracker. He restrained it, but only just, before he spoke in a deep husky voice which seemed to reverberate in her abdomen.

'Where were *you* the morning after?' he said, not bothering to answer a single one of her perfectly reasonable questions.

'I... I needed to get to Kildare and you weren't there. You'd gone off on another joyride, if you recall.'

'Joyride?' He laughed, the sound doing nothing to quell the heated glow in her abdomen. 'Is that what we're calling it?'

'What else would you call it?'

'Nuts? Dangerous? Wild? Exciting?' he murmured, and she realised he was referring to the ride they had taken together. The one she didn't want to talk about, but now somehow was. The fact that it was making the glow in her stomach jiggle and jive could not be good. 'But joyful?' he said. 'Nah, I don't think so. If it was joyful, I wouldn't have been left with an ache I couldn't satisfy. And you wouldn't have high-tailed it out of there the next morning as if your butt was on fire.'

The blush hit the top of her head and the soles of her feet simultaneously. 'I... I apologised for that ache.'

Fury flared again in those true-blue eyes and she knew she'd hit a nerve. Again.

'And I told you I didn't want your apology,' he ground out.

'What *do* you want then?' she blurted out, and realised her mistake immediately when he reached out and skimmed his thumb down her cheek. Before she could stop herself, she leaned into the caress.

She yanked herself back, but it was already too late because he'd noticed.

He dropped his hand, buried it in the pocket of his jeans, but she could still feel his touch and the brutal hunger ready to drive her to do stupid things.

'What do *I* want?' he said as if he were seriously considering the question. 'I want you to stop lying to yourself and me. And I want you to stop running.'

'I wasn't the one who disappeared for four days,' she countered, drowning now and willing to throw anything at him to escape the incontrovertible truth that there was going to be no going back to the way they had been. He had seen who she really was that night—reckless, impulsive and pathetically needy—and he wasn't going to let that girl hide behind the appropriate, the polite, the professional again.

A part of her hated him for demolishing all her defences so easily. But she hated herself more—for giving him that power. For letting him see behind the façade she had built so carefully, and which had protected her for so long. Until now.

'Fair point,' he said with a nonchalance that scared her.

How could her emotions be so raw and his be so calm, so controlled?

'Can't you just forget about that kiss?' she

asked, hearing the pleading note and hating herself even more.

'Nope, I can't forget it,' he said with an acceptance that only pushed her closer to the edge. But then he added, 'Can you?'

'Of course I can,' she said, but she already knew she was lying.

And she had an awful suspicion he knew she was lying too.

CHAPTER TEN

'BY THE WAY, Jamilla, we must pick a gown for you to wear at the Paris ball before you leave,' Orla suggested as she tucked into the delicately marinated chicken which was one of the few things she could eat without upsetting her stomach. 'We can have it altered for you when you get there.'

Jamilla blinked and stared at her friend. Then her gaze shot to Dane, only to find him watching her—like a hawk. Or, rather, a wolf.

Oh, no. She'd mentioned borrowing a gown to attend the ball a week ago without telling Orla about her bargain with Dane. But she had no intention of accompanying him to the lavish event now. Not after their kiss, and the media furore she'd just spent four days trying to get under control.

'I don't think that will be necessary now,' she said, concentrating on cutting the steak she'd been served, which she had been struggling to eat since she'd sat down at the large dining table.

She'd debated not coming down to supper at all, after the way her 'meeting' with Dane had ended earlier. But she'd forced herself to put in an appearance. She didn't want to give him any more ammunition. Didn't want him to think she was running scared. Even if she was. But now she wished she'd chickened out. Because anything would be better than the tangle of nerves playing tag with the few bites of steak she'd actually managed to swallow.

'Are you sure?' Orla said, unaware of the real reason Jamilla had agreed to attend the ball with Dane. 'I think it's a great idea to have you take a more visible role. You've spent months co-ordinating the tour and no one's more knowledgeable than you about the trade mission. I think you'll be a major asset when it comes to meeting with the ministers and dignitaries that are due to attend.'

'I've briefed Dane extensively,' she murmured, giving Orla a pointed look. 'I'm sure he'll do an excellent job of representing the kingdom,' she finished.

After his four-day disappearing act and his insistence on talking about everything *but* the job they had to do that afternoon, she wasn't convinced any more that he was remotely committed to their goal. But, right now, she didn't care.

One thing she did know—she absolutely

couldn't go to the ball on his arm. It would only reawaken the frenzied publicity about their kiss, which she'd been trying to crush. Not to mention her hyperactive hormones, which appeared to be incapable of distancing themselves from the events of that night too.

'While your sudden confidence in me is appreciated, Jamilla,' Dane said, his gaze fixed on her face with the intensity of a laser beam, sarcasm dripping off every word, 'I doubt I'll be able to do as good a job schmoozing those stiffs as you.'

The blush she'd been managing to suppress—ever since she'd arrived in the salon for their meal and seen him shaved and showered, wearing a fresh pair of dark jeans and a cashmere sweater that clung to his chest like a second skin—bloomed across her cheeks like a mushroom cloud.

She'd never been a blusher. Now she couldn't seem to stop blushing.

'But if you're too scared to accompany me the way we agreed…?' he added, the implication unmistakable.

She slammed down her knife and fork, forgetting their audience, forgetting everything but the man across from her, his challenging gaze calling her a coward. *Again.*

'I'm not scared of you,' she hissed, the stress finally releasing its stranglehold on her throat.

'Sure you are—you're terrified of admitting you still want me,' he said.

She blinked, so incensed now she could barely breathe. How dare he say that in front of Orla, in front of Karim? But it wasn't the thought of her employers that was making the temper start to choke her, it was that smug expression on his face and the way it made her feel. Angry, on edge and impossibly aroused.

'I don't still want you,' she insisted.

'Yeah, you do,' he said. 'Or you wouldn't have all but melted into a puddle at my feet an hour ago when I touched you.'

Karim cleared his throat loudly, sending his brother a baleful look and yanking Jamilla back to reality.

Jamilla's blush became fiery. 'I'm so sorry, Your Majesty,' she mumbled, wishing she could melt into the floor and disappear. 'I forgot myself.'

She'd been sparring with Dane like a surly teenager— at the dinner table, in front of the King and Queen. The sort of mouthy, opiniated teenager she'd never been.

Dane, of course, didn't look remotely apologetic or even concerned. If anything, he looked even more smug. And even more gorgeous. *Drat the man.* Did appearances, propriety, appropriate behaviour mean nothing to him?

'There's no need to address me by my title

here, Jamilla,' Karim murmured. 'And please don't apologise.' He sighed. 'My brother tends to have that effect on everyone.'

'Thanks, bro,' Dane said, clearly not bothered by the observation in the least. He was still watching her, his lips curving on one side into a cynical grin. A grin that was as good as calling her a liar. 'What you guys don't know, because I guess she didn't tell you, is that we had a deal, Jamilla and I. A deal she's now too scared of a little press attention to follow through on.'

'It won't be a small amount of press…' she began, but he simply lifted his hand, silencing her. And sending her temper through the roof.

'The deal was I'd wear the dress uniform of the Zafari head of state if she agreed to back me up at the ball. But, hey, it's no skin off my nose. I'd much rather wear something that doesn't make me look like a phoney. And I'm sure I can wing it with the trade ambassadors if I have to. It's pretty clear Jamilla's scared she won't be able to resist me if she comes to the ball as my date.'

Indignation poured through her like molten lava at his goading words, turning the longing in her chest into a hot lump of outrage. It plunged deep into her abdomen like a comet—making her so mad she was surprised she didn't leap across the table and wring his neck.

He'd made her look like an unprofessional

fool in front of people who she respected—
people who mattered to her. He had insisted on
bringing up their intimate relationship *again*,
when she'd done everything in her power to de-
flect and deny and mitigate the fallout from that
night. The way it needed to be deflected and denied and mitigated.

'You arrogant jerk…' She sucked in a breath
past the stick of gelignite now lodged under her
breastbone and all but choking her. 'I'll have no
trouble at all resisting you.'

'Prove it,' he murmured.

Her temper snapped like a dry twig. 'Fine…
I will.' She turned to Orla, who was watching
them both with undisguised interest. 'If you're
still happy for me to borrow one of your gowns,
I'd be more than happy to take a more visible
role at the ball. And schmooze the trade ministers to within an inch of their lives.' She shot
her searing gaze back to Dane. 'But that means
you have to wear the uniform.'

The curve of his lips became a devastating
smile. 'Happy to,' he said and tucked back into
his steak, but the smug smile had kicked up several notches.

And suddenly she knew she'd just handed him
the outcome he'd wanted all along.

Jamilla, you fool.

CHAPTER ELEVEN

'YOUR HIGHNESS, MS ROUSSEL is ready to accompany you.'

Dane turned in the ornate antechamber of the Zafari embassy in Paris at the hushed comment from his valet Hakim. His breath clogged in his lungs. And the heat which was never far away when he was near his chief diplomatic aide flared.

Damn.

His gaze roamed over the exquisite and intricately beaded gown of raw red silk, the demure but somehow erotic neckline which exposed just a hint of cleavage. The whisper-thin gauzy material that floated over the silk did nothing to disguise Jamilla's high breasts, her slender waist, the flare of her hips and her mile-long legs.

At last his gaze rose to her face. The tumble of glossy black curls had been corralled by a jewelled tiara, adding the final regal touch to the dramatic display. Her wide amber eyes, made to look even bigger by expertly applied eyeliner and the golden glitter on her lids, flashed with a rare fire.

The flush of colour only made her look more incredible. More stunning.

And every inch a queen.

The tiara's jewels glinted in the light of the antechamber's chandelier as she stepped forward. Her gaze flitted over him, the flash of a desire she couldn't hide only making the temper in her eyes more arousing.

He adored the bold fury on her face, he realised, even if it was directed at him.

He strode towards her, the sound of the ceremonial sword on his hip clinking, and for the first time let the feeling of power and majesty flow through him unchecked.

When he had first looked at himself in the mirror ten minutes ago—decked out in the ceremonial uniform of Zafar's head of state—he had felt like an imposter, the sight of the ornate and imposing outfit reminding him uncomfortably of his father. Arrogant, cold, untouchable.

It had not been a good moment.

But as he'd continued to stare at his reflection, instead of seeing the man who had ruled Zafar for so long with an iron fist, the man he barely remembered, he began to see his brother Karim. A good man, a good brother and as much a part of his past, a part of who he was, as the man who had never wanted him. Karim, who had not only stood by him as a boy but had stood up for his people, his country, and taken on so much. A true king.

And the uniform which he'd considered a foolish costume had become something more— a symbol of family, of heritage, of legacy. A royal legacy he had never felt a part of, but he could see now—thanks in no small part to the work of the stunning woman standing in front of him, frowning—he could honour for at least one night, if he let that feral, unloved kid go.

He took Jamilla's hand in his and bent at the waist to bring her fingers to his lips. He felt her jolt of shock and glanced up to see her eyes darken to a rich gold as he kissed her knuckles.

'You look like a queen,' he said as he straightened, not bothering to hide the husky desire in his voice. 'It suits you.'

The colour in her cheeks heightened, making the smooth skin glow. Her throat flexed as she swallowed heavily. 'Except I'm not a queen. You, on the other hand…' she murmured, repeating the line he'd once fed her at the oasis as she sent him a pointed look and he saw the awareness she couldn't hide shadow her eyes.

He let out a rough chuckle, stupidly pleased by her obvious appreciation despite her attempts to maintain her temper. He wasn't a king, not even close. But tonight, for once, he refused to be an outcast. He planned to play the role he'd been assigned to the hilt. Not just to stick it to the man who had rejected him all those years ago, but also to turn the residual flash of temper in those rich amber eyes to something more enjoyable.

He wanted her; she knew that. And he was through playing nice—they'd had six full days in Paris, dancing around each other, the changes she'd made to the schedule conveniently keeping her clear of him most of the time. But he'd bided his time, knowing that tonight she wouldn't be able to avoid him. And now he had her where he wanted her, he intended to use every weapon in his arsenal to hear those soft sobs again and make her soar.

He forced himself to bank the hunger which had been building for over a week, recalling that he had several hours of industrial strength schmoozing to get through first.

He offered his elbow and after a brief hesitation she placed trembling fingertips on his forearm. She looked unsure but determined. The flames in his gut turned into a bonfire.

He loved that she was so transparent, but what he loved more was that she had finally lost the façade of propriety, no longer able to deny the energy sparking between them like an electrical force field.

He led her out of the antechamber onto the

mezzanine level, heard her breathing accelerate as the lavish ballroom came into view.

A footman bowed and the ripple of conversation, the tinkle of champagne flutes and the ambient music below them fell silent.

'*Son altesse le Prince Dane Jones de Zafar, et Mademoiselle Jamilla Omar Roussel.*' The usher announced them in French, then English, then Zafari.

The hushed expectation of the crowd was broken by a spontaneous round of applause as bulbs flashed and the ripple of welcome became a roar.

The whispers rose to a crescendo as the eyes of the crowd devoured the spectacle they made— defiant, proud and, in Jamilla's case, hot as hell.

He could imagine the gossip columns going nuts tomorrow, devoting every column inch to the beautiful woman on his arm, but tonight she was his.

As they made their way down the wide sweeping staircase he leaned towards Jamilla, the lungful of her scent making the heat in his abdomen flare, and whispered in her ear, 'Time to knock 'em dead, Your Fake Majesty.'

The throaty laugh that burst out of her mouth, breaking the tension he could feel radiating off her, made him feel like a real prince for the first time in his life.

'Absolutely, Zafar is keen to participate on the world stage in a meaningful way. We have initiatives in place to ensure that our climate goals are met while we expand our agricultural output,' Jamilla said to the German MEP who had been quizzing her for the last ten minutes.

'I'd love to see what those initiatives are,' the older woman said, but then she smiled. 'I must say, I'm impressed, Ms Roussel, after the…' She paused, then coughed slightly, sending Jamilla an apologetic look. 'After the publicity in Rome about the tour I had assumed the title of Chief Diplomatic Aide was a euphemism for something else entirely. I apologise.'

Jamilla's cheeks burned. The woman had said what she knew a lot of other people at the ball were probably thinking. It had bothered her greatly, especially when she'd put on the borrowed gown for the first time and seen how it lifted her breasts and clung to her curves, making her recall the blurred paparazzi shots of her and Dane wrapped around each other. In that moment she had felt like a courtesan, not a queen.

She was used to standing back, to being invisible at events like this. She was there to support and advise, not to take a visible role.

She had wanted to hate Dane for putting her in this position and turning the tour into even more of a media circus than it was already. But as the evening had worn on and she'd found herself talking to a series of diplomats and politicians, civil servants and their spouses, using her linguistic skills and her vast knowledge of Zafar's new agricultural and cultural programmes, she had begun to gain confidence. Not least because, much to her astonishment, rather than belittling her or talking over her, Dane had remained by her side for the first portion of the evening and had been surprisingly encouraging and supportive.

Of course, having him there and being aware of every shift of his body, every waft of his scent, every look he sent her—full of heat and approval—had also kept her on edge, the bomb in her stomach which had begun ticking as soon as she'd laid eyes on him in the honorary uniform now ready to explode. But she didn't resent it any more. Or not as much.

They were doing a good job together. The speculation about their personal relationship had only enhanced the tour's visibility—and she could do damage limitation tomorrow when she returned to her backroom role.

'Thank you, I think,' she said, giving a half laugh.

She caught sight of Dane about fifteen feet away through the crowd, more at ease now. He'd lost the sword when they'd gone into dinner, just as she had lost her tiara, but he still looked tall and indomitable and commanding and every inch a prince as he spoke to a group that included Zafar's French ambassador, an EU trade minister and a high-ranking British civil servant. She had no idea what he was saying to them, probably not any of the talking points she'd spent months working on, but she suspected, whatever it was, it was going to increase Zafar's profile exponentially.

The man was a born networker—charismatic, ridiculously gorgeous but also with that cool, edgy confidence and don't-give-a-damn attitude which made people gravitate towards him and hang on his every word.

'He is an exceptional ambassador for his country,' the MEP all but purred beside her. 'I am surprised the King has not called on his services before. On *both* your services; you make a very attractive couple,' the woman added.

Jamilla felt the heat in her cheeks flare. 'We're not a couple,' she said.

And Karim has called on my services; in fact I've been doing this job for years.

She bit down on her resentment. The woman had no reason to know who she was, because she had always been invisible before. 'I'm just here to support His Highness for the duration of the tour,' she added when the woman simply smiled as if they shared a particularly juicy secret.

'Your blush—and those photos—tell a different story,' the MEP said, the confidential smile kind rather than judgemental.

'That was… That was just a moment of madness,' she said, regurgitating the line she'd been trying to sell for over a week to explain her lapse of judgement. But she wasn't sure she was convincing anyone any more. Not even herself. 'Rome is a very romantic city, it was late and we got a little carried away.'

'Pourquoi mentir, ma chérie, alors qu'il est évident pour tout le monde que vous couchez avec lui?'

She stiffened and swung round at the rude comment, the deep French accent laced with amused contempt.

Why lie, my dear, when it is obvious to everyone you are sleeping with him?

A slim man of medium height in a dress uniform with some medals clipped to the breast, his handsome face lined with age and his chestnut hair grown white at the temples, stood behind her. His gaze raked over her and the amused contempt turned to a grudging, but much more disturbing, respect.

'Jamilla,' he said, switching to English as the German politician excused herself discreetly. 'You look as…' he paused to let his gaze roam over her again, making her feel both exposed and unseen '…as beautiful as your mother.'

Jamilla's frantic heartbeat hit her tonsils, the

wrenching pain of memory exploding in her skull, of the last time she had seen this man, and he had tugged her small arms from around his waist and told her in stern French she needed to stop making such a fuss, that he would come and visit her, but only if she had learned to behave herself.

A tidal wave of confused, and confusing, emotions—shock, desperation, hope, fear, humiliation—blindsided her, but beneath it all was the sickening undertow of worthlessness which had dogged her throughout her childhood.

And the word she had whispered like a prayer each night before she fell asleep, as she'd kissed the faded, creased photograph she'd kept hidden under her pillow for years after that hideous day, spilled out of her mouth again.

'Papa…?'

'Could I give you my card, Your Highness?' the snooty British bureaucrat asked him. 'I think the Minister for Media and Culture would love to invite you to London.'

'Sure.' Dane took the card, knowing he had no intention of adding another date to the tour, but Jamilla could figure out how to tell the guy. He tucked the card into his back pocket and bid the man goodbye, then strode off before he could get waylaid again.

Where was she? They'd been at this charm

offensive for hours. Through six courses of cordon bleu cuisine in the banqueting hall next door after the initial reception, then back in the ballroom for another go-round of tedious small talk. Surely they could leave now. He was tired of schmoozing, tired of being on his best behaviour, and he wanted to get back to that heated look in her eyes. The one she'd been busy trying to bank all evening.

Luckily, at six three he was taller than most of the people in the room. His gaze swept over the heads of the exclusive crowd, the music from a French marching band getting on his last nerve, then zeroed in on her like an Exocet missile.

Wait a minute. Something's not right.

He could feel the tension radiating off Jamilla even from across the ballroom.

He strode towards her, pushing his way through the crowd, ignoring the offered greetings, the obsequious bows. Then she turned and he could see her expression.

Concern pumped and twisted in the pit of his stomach.

She looks...devastated.

Then he noticed the guy standing in front of her, an older man in a uniform. The man was talking to her but she looked stricken and she wasn't talking back. Which was even more wrong. Because if there was one thing Jamilla knew how to do it was talk, even when she was freaking out. He ought to know.

At last he got close enough to catch the end of what the guy was saying.

'Don't be embarrassed, my dear. Your mother knew the value of using sex to get what she wanted. And I'm sure Prince Dane appreciates it.'

The words slammed into him, insulting, contemptuous and just plain wrong. But beneath it was a spike of guilt, propelling his temper from zero to ninety in five seconds flat.

Reaching them, he didn't think, didn't stop to consider their audience or their mission. He grabbed the jerk by the lapels of his fancy jacket, yanked him up to his toes and shoved his nose into the guy's face. 'What the hell did you just say to her, you son of a...?'

'Dane, please, it's okay,' Jamilla said, grasping his forearm, but her fingers were shaking and her skin had become ashen.

'No, it's not okay,' he shouted, shoving the guy away from him. The man sent him an outraged look, brushed off his uniform, but then, noticing their growing audience, he disappeared into the crowd. Dane wanted to chase after the guy, but he couldn't leave Jamilla.

'No one gets to talk to you like that.' He held her waist, felt the convulsive shudder and saw the devastation in her eyes she couldn't disguise. 'No one.'

She flinched, bowed her head, the colour flooding back into her cheeks, probably because lights were flickering on around them as people held up their phones to record the scene.

To hell with them. If they wanted to splash this all over social media they could. He wasn't letting her go until he'd banished the distress from her eyes.

'Let's get out of here,' he said, and she nodded.

He put his arm around her waist and led her through the crowd, shielding her from the camera phones, ignoring the shouted intrusive questions from the scattering of press still at the event. Their security joined them, providing a phalanx of protection, holding the onlookers back as he headed up the stairs to the mezzanine.

Why hadn't she called that old bastard out herself? Where was the strong woman he knew her to be? The strong, smart woman who had the guts of a lion and who, even when she was freaking out about propriety and appearances and all the stuff she'd made it her job to manage, could still cut through him with a single look?

By the time they had reached the floor where their suites were located—and he had dismissed the security detail—she looked fragile and broken. And she was still shaking.

Alone at last, he led her into the sitting room

of his suite. She drew away from his hold and walked to the large multi-paned window, wrapping her arms around her waist as if she were trying to contain the pain. He forced himself not to follow her as she stood staring out at the carpet of lights which was the Marais at night.

He crossed his arms over his chest, his heart still thundering in his ears. He wanted to punch something, but more than that he wanted to hold her—until the shudders of reaction still coursing through her body went away. But the urge to comfort her scared him almost as much as seeing her so broken. When had his obsession with her become more than just sexual, more than just a physical need?

After several painful moments she stopped trembling and turned towards him. She'd composed herself and put the mask he hadn't seen for a while back on. But he could see the effort it was costing her to keep it in place.

'I'm sorry I got you involved in that,' she said, her voice firm but her eyes filled with shadows. His temper sparked. She hadn't involved him; he'd involved himself. Whatever the heck had just happened, the only person who wasn't to blame was her.

But he suppressed the knee-jerk reaction to point that out to her because she looked as if a strong breath would knock her down.

'You should return to the reception...' she

continued in that firm, *too* firm, voice. 'I will work on a response for the press for this incident...'

'To hell with the press,' he said, cutting her off. Because there was only so much of that hollow, haunted look he could stand. 'Who *was* that guy?' he demanded, suddenly wanting to know. Why did that guy have the power to devastate her?

She blinked slowly, then her lips lifted in a smile that didn't come close to touching the agony in her eyes. 'That was Lieutenant-Colonel François Xavier Roussel, formerly of the French army, now a retired diplomat,' she said. 'I should have realised he might have been included on the ambassador's guest list and been better prepared.'

'Roussel?' he said, his eyes narrowing as he ignored her latest attempt to take the blame for that bastard's smutty comments. 'Is he related to you?'

She drew in a ragged breath, but her gaze finally connected with his—and he could see the woman he'd come to desire finally flicker back to life.

'He's my father.'

Jamilla watched fury cross Dane's face like a thundercloud, before he swore profusely. 'That bastard is your old man?'

She flinched but, strangely, the violent reaction and the outrage darkening his expression released her from the dazed fog which had sucked her in ever since she had turned in the ballroom to see the man whose respect she had once longed for, with that disdain on his face she had never forgotten and in some small corner of her heart had always believed she deserved.

Dane had charged in, looking every inch the conquering warrior he was born to be, and had protected her against that man and that look and that feeling which had always lurked inside her—that she was worthless. That somehow she was to blame for her father's neglect, and her mother's sadness after he had left them and refused to return.

'Why would he talk to you like that about your sex life?' Dane said, his outrage gathering pace. 'Like some kind of creepy pervert?'

A brittle laugh burst from her, Dane's confusion almost as compelling as his outrage. The pain in her ribs released and she sucked in her first full breath in over twenty minutes, making her body feel buoyant. And free.

In his own fierce, formidable, reckless, impulsive and completely inappropriate way, Dane had given her this—the freedom to finally know, *really* know, she had never been to blame for the bad, selfish, dishonourable choices her father had made, or the way her mother had faded and eventually died because of them.

'What's so damn funny?' he said, but his gaze

had softened and she could see the relief in his eyes too.

She covered her mouth, another chuckle bubbling out on the wave of release and euphoria. Maybe the laugh was a little manic, a little desperate, and she was going to have regrets about the scene downstairs tomorrow morning—when she was doing major damage limitation with the press, *again*. But all she could see right now was the horrified shock in her father's eyes as Dane had hauled him up to his toes. All she could think about was the ludicrous irony—that her father had accused her of being a whore when she'd never slept with any man, let alone Dane— and all she could feel was gratitude that Dane had been there to protect her when she hadn't been able to protect herself.

'Honestly?' she replied. 'The absolute shock on his face when you told him what a jerk he was.'

'Yeah? Well, he earned it.' His lips twisted in a sensual smile which only made his harshly handsome features more gorgeous.

Adrenaline pumped through her system, chased by the familiar wave of heat. But this time, instead of trying to deny it or contain it, she stepped forward and lifted up on her tiptoes to cup his cheek. 'Thank you, Dane, for coming to my rescue.'

He frowned, but his hands landed on her hips

and caressed through the whisper of silk. The flare of desire in his gaze made her heart do a giddy little two-step and heat surged.

'Be careful, Jamilla,' he murmured, the tone husky with warning, the twinkle of amusement gone. 'I've wanted to finish what we started ever since Rome.' His gaze drifted down to her lips and the desire swelled and glowed at her core, releasing a rush of moisture and making the giddy two-step turn into hard, heavy thuds that pounded in her sex and echoed in her chest. 'Hell, long before that, if I'm honest.' He sighed. 'And I'm not great with deferred gratification. So you need to back off, unless you want to finish this too.'

She should have been terrified by the hot purpose in his eyes, and the solid ridge in his trousers pressing against her belly. And the tense line of his jaw, telling her how much it was costing him not to take what she was offering.

But the elemental desire to mate was nothing compared to the surge of longing, of need, in her heart. Maybe he didn't do deferred gratification, but he'd done it for her.

'I... I want to finish what we started in Rome too,' she said, her words guttering out on a husky breath as she wound her arms around his neck and pressed her curves against him, cradling the hard ridge against her belly and making the melting spot between her thighs burn.

His hands rose up her torso—rough, calloused, desperate, but somehow still restrained—to lift the heavy fall of hair from her neck and cradle her head. He raised her chin to study her with an intensity that stole her breath. The surge of hunger was nothing compared to the chaotic clamour of her heartbeat as she saw the passion she had long denied reflected in the deep blue depths of his irises.

'Just to be clear, I'm no one's knight in shining armour. If that's what you're looking for, I'm not that guy.'

But you are. You were my knight tonight. The first person ever to stand up for that little girl who thought she didn't deserve her father's love.

She tried to clamp down on the fanciful, romantic notion, but it whispered through her heart regardless. Poignant, powerful, needy, but also somehow so right.

'You need to be sure?' he finished. 'Because sex is all I've got to offer.'

It wasn't true.

She'd seen him with his brother, his nephew, his sister-in-law, had known the struggle to fulfil the role they'd asked of him was much harder than he had ever let on. But he'd done it because he loved them.

And she knew all about the little boy who had written so many letters to a father who had never been worthy of him.

He had so much more to offer than he realised. But she also knew it would be foolish to believe the person he would offer it to would be her.

'I am sure,' she said, emotion clogging her throat as her pulse jumped, giddy with anticipation.

There would be a price tomorrow—that she would pay, and he would not. There was a reason she hadn't taken this step before, with another man. But she would pay that price willingly, so she didn't have to step back again. She wanted to test her newfound freedom and finally let that girl go for good—the one who had always been so cautious, so careful, looking for acceptance and approval where there was none.

Tonight she would revel in the heat, the power of just grabbing what she wanted with both hands and not thinking, not feeling, not even caring about the consequences.

He swore softly, then bent to lift her into his arms.

Her heart leapt as she clung to his neck and the weight in her chest sank deep into her abdomen and throbbed—insistent, painful, but so real, so raw, so vivid.

As he strode into the bedroom with her in his arms she knew she was fully alive, fully seen, fully herself for the first time in her life.

She revelled in the heady excitement as

he dragged off her dress, the whisper of silk against her over-sensitised skin turning the flickering flames into an inferno, and ignored the visceral tug of fear caused by the possessive light in his eyes.

CHAPTER TWELVE

WHOA.

Dane had to stop from swallowing his own tongue as the silk gown gathered in a pool at Jamilla's feet. She stood proud in a couple of tantalising wisps of purple lace, but he could still see the beguiling flush of awareness, the shudder of a response as his gaze roamed over her curves.

The heat in his guts clamoured for release, insistent and barely controlled. The erection turned to iron.

He forced himself to take a breath, to stem the need to rip off the lace, to devour every gorgeous inch, plunge deep inside her and claim her as his.

Chill out. Control it. You're not an untried kid any more.

He couldn't keep her, didn't want to own her in anything other than a carnal sense. And this one night would have to be enough. Because, in some distant part of his heart, he already knew she'd come to mean more to him…to know him better…than any other woman ever had, or could. And that scared him.

But if they only had one night he wanted it to be good, for both of them. Even if he couldn't keep her, he never wanted her to forget him.

He traced a fingertip over the swell of her breast, watched the dark nipple tighten.

'Take off the bra,' he demanded, knowing he couldn't risk doing it himself or he might tear it from her.

The flush deepened, her eyes dark with desire, but also wary. Reaching behind her, she hesitated, then the loud snap of the hook releasing echoed around the room and the lace dropped from her arms.

The heat became painful as he devoured the sight of her high, firm breasts. Lush and full and begging for his attention.

Her arms folded over the swollen flesh, and his gaze snapped to hers. He saw the wariness, the need, mixed together. And it only made the ache in his pants—to claim her, to brand her—stronger and more volatile.

'What's the problem?' he forced himself to ask. Because beneath the desire in those enchanting amber eyes he could see something else. Not fear, exactly, but definitely something he would never have expected from her…vulnerability.

'I… I want to see you naked too,' she said, her hesitation only making the heat spread.

His wry laugh came out on a gruff rumble. 'Sure,' he said. It took him less than ten seconds to slip off his shoes, tug off the uniform jacket, the shirt, then rip open his trousers and kick them off with his shorts.

Her gaze dipped, shock flickered, but perversely that look only made the heat pound harder in his sex. He knew he wasn't a small guy—women had commented on it before. But something about the brutal flush made him want to reassure her. To reassure himself. That the need was something he could control, even though the effort to hold back was tougher now than it had ever been. And it reminded him of that frantic feral kid who had believed sex could fill all the empty spaces inside him.

He stepped closer, trapped himself against her belly and clasped her chin to lift her face to his. 'It's okay,' he said, his voice rough. 'We can take this slow.'

He watched her throat, that long slender neck contract as she swallowed heavily, felt his own throat dry up at the mix of timidity and determination in her gaze.

'Thank you,' she said. 'I would appreciate that.'

His lips quirked, her weirdly polite response breaking some of the tension.

Stepping back, he took her hands in his, drew

her arms away from her magnificent breasts. Her breath hitched but she made no move to cover herself again.

Leaning down, he captured one plump peak between his lips, licked and nipped, then flicked his tongue across the turgid tip.

She gasped, shuddered and thrust her fingers into his hair, caressing his scalp, her panting urging him on. He moved from one breast to the other, then reached down to slide searching fingers under the lace that covered her sex.

His breath stuttered, his own need like a comet, building and burning in his groin when he found her soaking wet.

He circled and stroked the plump nub, holding her neck with his other hand, lifting her chin to suckle the pounding pulse beneath her ear, which he had waited an eternity to exploit again. She moaned. He pushed one finger inside her, still circling, still stroking with his thumb, the sound of her sobs like a siren call to his senses as she gripped him. The thrill of seeing her shatter for him again made the need in his gut turn to burning pain.

He had to have her—now—or he would be lost for ever, the driving hunger threatening to reveal the needy boy all over again.

Jamilla cried out, the orgasm slamming into her like a freight train, so hard, so relentless, so unstoppable.

This was so much more than before. The stunning sensations exploded through her nerve-endings on a never-ending wave, but right behind it was a terrifying vulnerability.

As the orgasm finally released its stranglehold on her body, fear gripped her heart.

She tried to think, tried to pull away, pull back, to protect herself. But all she felt was raw and desperate need as he scooped her trembling body into his arms. She clung to his neck, still shivering, still shaken, every part of her limp and exposed as he cradled her shattered body as if she were precious, important.

He laid her on the bed, climbed over her, the huge erection brushing her thigh as he lifted her wrists above her head, pinned her hands to the bed. His startlingly blue eyes stared down at her, his breathing as ragged and raw as her own, the longing fierce and unfettered.

For a brief terrifying moment the brutal feeling of connection gripped her, but then he took her hips in his hands, angled her pelvis and placed the head of his erection at her entrance.

He pressed in slowly but surely, so large, so demanding, stretching the unbearably tight sheath, then thrust through the final barrier.

He grunted as the pinch of pain made her wince.

He swore, his gaze flying back to hers, the harsh look ripping away that delirious moment of connection—to replace it with accusation, and horrified shock.

She should have told him, she realised, about her virginity. It hadn't really occurred to her that he would want to know. It had felt private, maybe even a little embarrassing.

But it was already too late to do anything about it because he was lodged deep inside her, the pulsing ache building again, despite the pain.

'Are you a virgin?' he demanded.

She wanted to hide from that accusing look, and the shame she suddenly felt. She hadn't meant to trick him, but somehow it felt as if she had.

She opened her mouth to reply, when he said, 'Don't lie.'

Her throat contracted and she was forced to nod.

He swore again, his fingers tightening on her hips, his whole body stiffening, but instead of pulling out, rolling away in disgust, as she had almost expected, he remained lodged inside her. She could feel him deep inside her body, stretching her unbearably, the pulse of him matching the thready, throbbing beat of her heart. Her laboured breathing and his sounded deafening in the room as her chest heaved with the weight suddenly crushing her ribs.

What had she done? Why did he look so stricken, so unhappy?

He dropped his head, his hair brushing her cheek. 'Damn,' he said, the word full of a shame she didn't understand.

She lifted a trembling hand to his cheek, felt the muscle twitch and tighten beneath her palm. 'What's wrong?' she asked.

His head rose at last, his gaze meeting hers. 'Everything,' he said, his expression so bleak it made the weight grow into a boulder, threatening to cut off her air supply.

'I've got to move,' he said before she could ask what he meant. 'Am I hurting you? Can you take more of me?'

She wasn't sure she could, the stretched feeling already overwhelming, but she nodded anyway, shocked when the tug of pleasure pulsed deep in her abdomen as he pulled out then pressed back.

She held on, her fingers digging into his shoulders, aware of his struggle to hold on, to hold back. His hips circled, rocked, establishing a slow, steady rhythm. Each new plunge forced her to take a little more. But the pleasure built regardless, despite the echo of pain. She concentrated on it as it spread, consuming the frantic jump of her heartbeat, lifting the unbearable weight as the relentless sensations battered her.

The wave threatened, tumbling towards her, faster and harder now.

His movements became less sure, less steady,

more frantic, more furious, but it didn't matter any more. The soreness was consumed by euphoria as the wave barrelled through her. Huge, wild, untamed, the hot pleasure pummelled her body as he grew larger still.

He yanked himself free just as she flew over the top of that high wide ledge, leaving her alone in her ecstasy.

The sticky heat of his seed pumped onto her belly as he collapsed into her arms.

What have I done?

Dane rolled away from the woman beside him, her tantalising scent invading his senses, the overwhelming climax still pulsing in his groin leaving him bruised and battered.

But probably not as bruised and battered as the woman he'd just pounded into like a mad man. No wonder she'd looked so wary when she'd seen him naked and fully aroused.

She should have told him she was a virgin. But, even as he wanted to be mad at her, a small voice inside him was shouting, *Don't kid yourself, man. No way would that have stopped you.*

He forced himself to move, get off the bed and walk into the bathroom, aware of the shakiness in his legs, the weightless feeling of unreality in his stomach, the brutal tug of afterglow doing nothing to diminish the black hole forming in his chest.

What the hell did you expect, you dumb son of a...?

He cut off the angry, pointless recriminations as he washed away the evidence of her innocence. And recalled the brave, determined look in her eyes before he'd plunged into her.

He'd taken something he couldn't give back. She should have told him. But did that really matter? Because he wasn't even sure he wanted to give it back, the need still like a wild thing inside him, the echo of that titanic orgasm holding his heart in a vice. And the consequences of what he'd done—of what they'd done—pushed at that empty space inside him that for one moment had been filled.

Everything was so messed up in his head. But something he never would have expected had reared its head when he'd torn through that slight barrier and realised the truth.

His honour. And hers. An honour he knew he had to defend. Or he would be nothing again.

He threw the washcloth, now stained with her virginity, into the trash. After wrapping a towel around his hips, he grabbed another washcloth off the vanity. He rinsed it through with warm water. A strange acceptance settled over him as he walked back into the bedroom.

No way was he running from this situation. Or her. Or his father would have been right to discard him all those years ago.

He'd always found it easy to shirk commitment; the desire to protect and possess was a totally new phenomenon for him. But it was still there nonetheless.

He caught Jamilla bent over by the bed with the sheet wrapped tightly around her naked body.

She shot upright, the torn purple lace he'd ripped away before plunging inside her clutched in her fist. 'I... I should go back to my own suite,' she said, a vivid blush spreading like wildfire over her collarbone and up her neck. 'Before anyone finds out I'm here,' she added.

He frowned, not appreciating the guilty flush or the panic in her eyes.

Her hair fell in artless disarray—the dark corkscrew curls mussed from their lovemaking bouncing as she swung around, searching for the rest of her clothing.

He struggled to keep his anger at bay. She was trying to run from him again, the way she had in Rome.

Yeah, that wasn't happening. They'd done what they'd done and now they needed to face the consequences. Consequences she had to be well aware of.

'It's a bit late for that, don't you think?' he murmured, his lips twisting into a smile that didn't have a heck of a lot of humour in it.

They had a big problem, for sure. He hadn't

even had the sense to use a condom. But he'd be damned if he was going to try and dodge this conversation.

'No, no, I don't think so,' she said, becoming frantic as she scooped up her bra, bent to pick up the red silk dress pooled on the floor. She held the clothing to her chest, still clutching the sheet in a death grip.

The evidence of her innocence, and the thought that he was most likely the first guy— the *only* guy—to see her naked sent another surge of possessiveness through him, which he made no attempt to control this time.

'If I leave now I can take the back stairs to my own suite,' she carried on, talking as if she were the diplomatic aide again, instead of the woman who had climaxed in his arms. 'And if there are any questions tomorrow we can just stonewall.' He strode towards her as she dipped her head to look for her shoes. 'I can work out a press release to explain the scene with my father. And no one will know for sure what happened after we left the event together. They certainly won't be able to prove...'

He snagged her wrist, halting the frantic quali- fications and her attempts to gather up her cloth- ing. Her head rose and her gaze locked on his. And what he saw—panic, guilt, shame—had anger mixing with a cocktail of other emotions in his gut. Protectiveness, possessiveness, for sure, but also a cast-iron determination he never would have expected, to own this situation.

No way was he letting her just pretend this hadn't happened. Because he refused to be ashamed of who he was and what they'd done.

He'd spent so much of his childhood being pushed aside, had become convinced he had no right to his heritage, but he'd be damned if he was going to let her push him aside too.

'Yeah, but *we'll* know,' he said softly, to control the spiky fury churning in his gut. And the spurt of desire as her pulse pummelled his thumb. 'You should have told me you were a virgin, Jamilla. But you didn't and now it's too late. You want to hide this from the press, go ahead, I don't care about that, but you're not sneaking out of this suite tonight.'

Her mouth dropped open, the shock on her face somehow even more devastating than the scent of her—sultry and spicy and hot as hell—and a tangle of emotions he didn't understand in his gut.

'But…' Jamilla stammered, her whole face exploding with the heat still pulsing in her sex. 'You can't be serious, Dane. If I stay tonight, even if we can keep it secret from the media, everyone here will know.'

'So what?' he murmured, the tight smile on

his lips defied by the intensity in his eyes. 'You ashamed of me? Of what we just did?'

'No, of course not…' She stared back at him, her knuckles whitening as she held the sheet to her breasts, to cover skin still alive with sensation. Her breathing accelerated. Was he joking? But he didn't look as if he were joking? He looked deadly serious. 'I just… I didn't expect…'

'What did you think? That I'd kick you out once I'd taken your virginity? How much of a bastard do you think I am?'

'No…no… That's not… I never meant to imply you have no honour…' she began frantically, realising she had insulted him when that had never been her intention. But then the furrows on his forehead relaxed.

'Good to know,' he said, seeming to take her denial at face value.

'I could resign my position,' she offered, the brutal leap of her heart at his determination not to deny their liaison only scaring her more.

She had been completely convinced when she had decided to take this step, this leap…that this encounter would be a one-night deal.

But even as she had accepted that reality, and had been prepared for the emotional fall-out afterwards, a foolish bubble of hope she hadn't even been aware of until this moment had formed.

'You *could* resign,' he said, letting go of her wrist to thrust impatient fingers through his hair. 'But as I've got no intention of letting you out of my sight until we know for sure you're not pregnant, I don't see the point.'

Pregnant?

The word detonated in her chest like a bomb, destroying the bubble of hope along with every ounce of her courage.

'But I'm… I can't be pregnant. You…you didn't…' Hot blood flooded into her cheeks. 'Inside me, you didn't…' she finished weakly, not even able to say the relevant words, feeling like a gauche, artless schoolgirl instead of the focused, capable career woman she had worked so hard to become.

'Are you using contraceptives?' he asked bluntly.

She shook her head, unable to say the words, the guilt as sharp as the feeling of inadequacy she'd once thought she could bury by jumping into his bed.

'Then there's still a chance. Even if I didn't ejaculate inside you,' he said, saying the words she'd been too embarrassed to say.

'I'm so sorry,' she said, realising this was why he felt honour-bound to make this more than one night. Perhaps he wasn't planning to propose, but she knew enough about him now, and his complex relationship with his father and his heritage, to be convinced he would never abandon her to handle this situation alone. 'I didn't think. I should have asked you to wear a condom.'

'Hey,' he murmured, tucking a knuckle under her chin. He lifted her face back to his. 'We were both carried away in the moment, Jamilla,' he said, his willingness to own the situation only making the tidal wave of shame toss and turn in her stomach.

He cradled her face, brushed his thumb over her lips in a gesture so intimate her breath released in a rush. 'We both should have had that conversation, and we didn't.'

She found herself brutally close to tears, needing to lean on his strength—if just for a moment.

How could he be so pragmatic about this? Shouldn't he be furious that she had put him, put them both, into this untenable position?

'I can take a test in the next few days to be sure,' she said, her voice almost as shaky as she felt.

He dropped his hand from her face to rest it on her waist. 'Where are you in your cycle?'

She swallowed at the blunt question, and the colour flared to her hairline.

Seriously, Jamilla? You slept with this man, had several mind-blowing orgasms, had him buried so deep inside you, you could feel him everywhere, and yet you've got a problem talking about your menstrual cycle with him?

'About midway through,' she managed. Then realised the significance of the timing. *Oh, God*, she could be ovulating. What if she actually did get pregnant…? He'd pulled out, but…

Before she had a chance to go into full-on panic mode, his hand squeezed her hip, drawing her back from the edge. 'Stop freaking out.'

She nodded, humbled—but also terrified—by his willingness to take charge, because it opened up that agonising yearning inside her, which had always longed for a man to protect her and care for her. She shouldn't need Dane's care or attention, shouldn't want it, because all it did was make her weak.

But, even so, it took a massive effort to step away from his touch.

She turned from his probing, intense gaze, her fist still clutching her torn underwear and the red silk dress she had worn without any intention of trapping a prince. Or so she'd wanted to think. But, right now, the situation—and his reaction to it—was making her feel brutally exposed.

To think she'd once believed *he* was the reckless one.

'I'm still sorry that I didn't tell you about my virginity,' she murmured as she gazed out of the window at the Parisian night. 'Or even think about contraception.' The Eiffel Tower looked resplendent in its majesty, a mile or so

away, rising like a tribute to the city's golden
age. She could even make out the dark ribbon
of the Seine, winding its way through the carpet
of lights. The magnificent view only made her
feel more insignificant—and overwhelmed by
everything that had happened in the last hour.
The last few weeks, in fact. She'd been impulsive and reckless tonight, had let that foolish,
fanciful girl free who had yearned so much for
male approval. And now look where she was.
She didn't feel like herself any more. Or at least
not the woman she'd wanted to be.

She forced herself to face Dane, brutally
aware of the insistent arousal as she took in
the ink on his shoulder blade and scrawled line
across his hip flexor, the ridged abs, the defined
muscles of his chest, the small raised scars she'd
glimpsed once before at the waterfall. So much
about him had surprised her, shocked her even,
but why hadn't she figured out until this moment
that she found every aspect of him intriguing,
captivating and utterly magnificent, even more
magnificent than the view behind her?

She sucked in a careful breath, scared even
more of what these feelings might mean. Was
she confusing sexual desire with intimacy? Was
this rush of feeling for Dane simply a by-product
of the emotional upheaval caused by the encounter with her father? It had to be, but how did she
stop it from getting worse?

'I don't want you to feel trapped into making this encounter more than it is,' she said, desperately trying to wrest back the control—and perspective—she had thrown away so carelessly.

He stepped towards her. 'I'll be the judge of that,' he murmured with a purpose that only frightened her more. 'We've got another seven days of this tour, right?' he asked. She nodded. 'Rather than source you a pregnancy test, which is bound to get out to the damn press, why don't we just get it done when we return to Zafar, if you haven't had your period already?'

'Okay,' she said, her lip trembling all of a sudden.

'Hey, stop it,' he said, taking a firm grip on her chin, to peer into her eyes. 'I'm not that bad a catch, am I?'

She sniffed loudly, not really appreciating what she was sure—was hoping—had to be a joke. She held the deluge back, terrified all over again by the treacherous feeling of connection pressing on her chest.

'I can't… We can't be a couple, not even if I get pregnant; that would be insane,' she said, suddenly terrified he might feel he had to propose, and that, given the turmoil of confused and confusing emotions currently churning in her stomach, she might not have the strength to reject him. Which would be wrong in every respect.

Her parents' marriage had ultimately been

one of convenience—for her father. From everything her mother had said about the events leading up to it, Jamilla could see he'd been pressured into marriage after he had seduced her mother. And in the end he had offered her his hand to protect his career in the diplomatic service as much as anything else. He had pretended to be in love. Had pretended to care for her mother. Had got her pregnant and then eventually abandoned them both, to return to the woman he really loved. She couldn't bear to be put in the same situation with Dane because he felt somehow beholden to her.

He raised a quizzical brow but didn't respond.

'I really think it would be best if I return to my own suite,' she said, but as she went to walk past him towards the en suite bathroom he grasped her upper arm.

'Nope,' he said.

Her foolish heart bounced up to become jammed in her throat. 'I don't think…'

'I told you already, I'm not letting you out of my sight,' he said, cutting into her frantic denials. 'How sore are you?' he added, the curt concern in his voice derailing her emotions all over again.

'More tender than sore, which is good considering how large…' She stopped abruptly when she realised what she'd almost blurted out.

Instead of looking offended, though, he let out a deep chuckle.

Her flush burned. 'I didn't mean to imply...' she began again. But it only made the wry chuckle turn into a laugh.

'Sure you did,' he said, his eyes bright with amusement at her expense. 'But it's okay. You're cute when you're flustered.'

Cute? She wasn't sure whether to be flattered or appalled at his comment but, before she had a chance to figure it out or get a hold on the last scrap of her already vastly diminished dignity, he turned her around to face the bathroom door and gave her a soft pat on the butt. 'Go grab a shower and when you're ready you can take the bed,' he said, letting her go. 'There's clean T-shirts in the dresser if you need something to sleep in. I'll see you tomorrow for breakfast in the sitting room.'

'But where will you sleep?' she asked, feeling stupidly bereft at the thought of spending the night alone in his bed.

Not that she was ready for more sex—she hadn't lied about being more than a little tender, in places she'd never been tender before.

'There's another bedroom on the other side of the sitting room. I think it's probably best if I crash in there until we head to Spain.' The hot assessing gaze skimmed over her burning skin, setting off a whole new set of bonfires en route. 'Your tender places are gonna need a chance to recover. And I need to source condoms without alerting the media.'

It wasn't until she was under the needle-sharp spray of the power shower ten minutes later, while every one of her erogenous zones throbbed in unison, that her nuclear blush finally began to subside. And it wasn't until she lay alone in his big bed, a good half-hour later, the soft cotton of the T-shirt she had found in his dresser cocooning her in the addictive scent of his laundry soap, that it occurred to her she hadn't corrected his high-handed assumption they were now an item for the duration of the tour. And would be sleeping together again.

As she snuggled into the luxury linen sheets and tried to turn off her racing brain, she promised herself she would correct him first thing tomorrow morning.

CHAPTER THIRTEEN

'SO WHAT'S THE deal with your old man?' Dane watched Jamilla's reaction intently as he dropped the question into their conversation over the lavish breakfast of crêpes and fruit and strong French coffee he'd ordered from the embassy kitchens.

Jamilla had been all business again as soon as she'd appeared from his bedroom that morning, or at least she'd tried to be all business, not that easy when she was wrapped in the suite's complimentary bath robe, her sleep-mussed curls riotous around her head and her fresh dewy skin devoid of her usual perfectly applied make-up.

He'd let her direct the conversation towards strategies for handling any press fallout from last night's events while their breakfast was delivered. And there would be fallout, because he'd already had to field a call from Karim, who had demanded to know what was going on.

He figured he didn't owe Karim an expla-

nation of his sex life. So he hadn't enlightened
him on the situation with Jamilla and how the
night had ended.

He guessed the smart move last night would
have been to help her sneak back to her own
rooms. He still wasn't entirely sure why he
hadn't, the urge to stand up for her, to get her
to stay, not making a whole lot of sense. But he
refused to second-guess it now, as he watched
her push her uneaten crêpes around her plate.
He clamped down on his annoyance at her attitude this morning.

If she wanted to keep their liaison secret
from the press, even from Karim and Orla, he
didn't have a problem with that, but he'd be
damned if he'd pretend last night had never
happened.

Maybe it was because of her virginity, perhaps it was about the possibility of a pregnancy, or maybe it was that spike of guilt when
he'd figured out the truth about her inexperi-
ence—the desire to prove he wasn't a man like
his father, who exploited women because he
could—but, whatever it was, he wasn't about
to change his mind. Plus he'd already figured
out that keeping a lid on this chemistry, which
had sparked between them the first time he'd
met her, was going to be impossible to contain
now so he didn't see the point of even trying.

They had a press conference scheduled for

later. Jamilla had already worked out a strategy for avoiding any intimate questions about their relationship. But he wanted to know why she'd shut down the way she had in front of her father.

His curiosity about her reaction was about more than just their dance with the media, though, especially when she stiffened and her gaze flicked away.

'It's not... There's not really a deal,' she said, making him even more sure there was a story and it was one he wanted to know about. Because he never wanted to see that look on her face again— stricken and shattered. 'To be honest, I hardly know him,' she continued. 'He left Zafar for good when I was six and never returned. But he wasn't around much before that. He lived mostly in Paris, even before my parents got divorced.'

'Wait a minute. So last night was the first time you'd seen him since you were a kid?'

She nodded and her gaze met his, then darted away again. But what he saw there—shame, embarrassment, guilt—had last night's anger building again.

The citrussy, buttery pancakes curdled in his stomach. The urge to throttle her father with his bare hands wasn't helped by the memory of the look in the bastard's eyes last night, when Dane had confronted him—arrogance and contempt—before he'd scuttled off into the crowd like the cockroach he was.

What kind of man wouldn't be proud to have Jamilla as a daughter?

He placed his knife and fork on his plate and struggled to even out his breathing, to stop the fury from taking hold again, his reaction only making him feel more exposed.

'It's probably best if we simply refuse to answer any questions about that incident,' she offered, placing her own utensils on her plate, next to the breakfast she hadn't eaten.

He already knew, from talking to Karim, the media were going to be all over her old man's appearance—not talking about it would only fuel the speculation. But, instead of correcting her, he went with instinct and placed his hand over the fist she had placed on the table.

Her gaze jerked to his. The naked emotion in her expression was quickly masked, but it still kicked him in the gut.

'He's a jerk, Jamilla. You deserved a better father.'

Her lips quivered slightly, the sheen of moisture in her gaze crucifying him even more. Because he knew her old man wasn't the only guy who didn't deserve her. He'd pounced on her last night, taken what he wanted... And after a sleepless night thinking about her response to him, that livewire connection, he knew his desire to keep her close for the next little while wasn't just about the possibility of pregnancy.

'I suppose we both did,' she said, so softly he almost didn't catch it.

'I guess,' he said, although he wasn't so sure. He'd been wild as a kid. Wild and untamed and unrestrained, and more than happy to use sex for comfort and validation as a teenager. Maybe most of the women he'd slept with back then had been a lot older than him, but he'd always been the one to walk away unscathed. And, however good they were together, he'd eventually do the same to Jamilla, assuming she wasn't carrying his baby right now. And if she was he would be unlikely to stick around for very long. Just long enough to give her and the child the protection of his name, and his wealth.

There was a knock on the door of the suite. He lifted his hand from hers, ignoring the strange tug in his chest as he stood to answer it.

The connection they shared could only be a sexual one. Maybe they'd both had crummy fathers, but while her daddy issues had created a brave, hard-working woman who'd held onto her innocence for far too long, his had created a guy who couldn't commit to anyone—while the only thing he'd been able to commit to was his business. That was his reality. He'd come to terms with it a long time ago. No point re-

gretting it now, when it was too late to change
who that boy had become.

'That'll be Hakim,' he said. 'I asked him to
speak to your assistant in confidence and have
her pack up your luggage and move it into this
suite for the duration of our stay.'

Wait—what?

Jamilla was still struggling to deal with the
catastrophic effect of Dane's consoling touch
as she listened to him answer the door. Luckily
the suite had an entry hall, so Hakim and her
assistant Kesia couldn't see her wearing nothing but a bathrobe and one of Dane's T-shirts
as they delivered her luggage and left. Even so,
she felt compromised and exposed when Dane
strode back into the room carrying one of her
suitcases. Her instinctive shiver of awareness
at the figure he cut in jeans and a T-shirt, the
day-old stubble on his jaw only making him
look more rugged, wasn't helping.

'Your assistant said your outfit for today is
in here,' he said.

'I can't stay here another night,' she said with
as much authority as she could muster as he
placed the suitcase in front of her.

He straightened, the devastatingly assured
movement making every one of her pulse
points throb painfully. 'Why not?' he asked,
as if he really didn't know.

'Because what if the press find out?'

'They won't. The staff know what happens in the embassy between us is strictly private,' he said.

'But it's not appropriate,' she sputtered. 'I work for you.'

'No, you don't,' he murmured. He stepped closer and cupped her cheek, then brushed his thumb across her lips, his gaze hot and intense and yet somehow also tender. Her heart melted, scaring her even more. 'You work for my brother,' he said. 'And he doesn't get to tell either one of us what to do in private.'

She ducked her head, scared to look at him. Scared of his certainty, his conviction. And the fierce possessiveness in his eyes.

'I can't…' She hesitated, attempted to swallow the bundle of anxiety wedged in her throat. 'I can't sleep with you again.'

'Do you mean you can't — or you don't want to?'

Her head jerked up, the riot of emotions painful in their intensity at the bold, unequivocal question. The longing worked its way up her torso and squeezed around her heart, the wave of need so strong she knew he had to be able to see it.

'You don't have to be a good girl any more, Jamilla,' he added, that deep husky voice coaxing the girl she'd tried so hard to control back out of hiding. 'Not for Karim, not for your bastard of a father. And certainly not for me.' He stroked her cheek, then let his hand fall. 'You're allowed to take what you want.' He pressed his hands into the back pockets of his jeans but his eyes remained fixed on her face, and she had the strangest sense he wasn't as sure or certain as he appeared. 'If you don't want me, I'll back off,' he said. 'But if you do... I say we enjoy this thing while it lasts. Or at least until we know for sure you're not pregnant.'

She heard the qualification. He wasn't offering anything permanent. Even if she were pregnant, she would be an obligation, nothing more. An obligation she had no intention of becoming. But the fierce longing was impossible to ignore.

Could she do it? Could she take him up on his offer? Let that bad girl loose for a little while longer, without regrets? And was there really any point trying to deny this urge any longer?

It would be a risk. A massive risk. Not just professionally—if the press found out the truth—but also personally. And a part of her was terrified she might be considering what he was offering her for all the wrong reasons. But another part of her—that reckless, impulsive part she'd rediscovered last night—pushed back against the fear. Until it turned into something insistent and impossible to ignore.

What would it be like to live in this moment without regrets? To, for once, leap before she looked? To do what felt good, instead of what felt sensible? She'd lived her whole life by rules—strict rules of decorum and denial—that she'd set for herself. And why? So she would be respected, admired, appreciated and be above reproach.

But most of all, deep down, so the man who had deserted her would know she was worthy to be his daughter. And now she finally understood, after last night, the dream she'd secretly been striving towards without even realising it would never come true.

Her father would never acknowledge her, never love her, no matter how faultless and perfect she was. So why was she still holding on for his approval? Hadn't she earned the chance to finally be herself? Truly herself? To tell Dane what she wanted, without regret? She'd always believed she'd remained a virgin for so long because the opportunity simply hadn't arisen to discover the sexual side of her being, but she knew now she'd simply been waiting. And, anyway, she wasn't a virgin any more.

'I do want you,' she said.

His lips quirked, the gleam in his eyes making her heart hammer against her chest wall. 'Then I say we go for it.'

She nodded. 'Oh…okay.'

He reached forward and clasped her around the waist. She grasped his shoulders, the weight in her chest lifting to butt against her tonsils as he lifted her into his arms.

When he let her down again, they were both grinning at each other like a couple of carefree kids with a naughty secret. The sort of carefree kids she suspected neither of them had ever been.

He clasped her cheeks, lifted her face to his and slanted his lips across hers, capturing the sob of need.

The kiss was deep, demanding, uncompromising, staking a claim to more than just her body, as his hands found the tie to the bathrobe and roamed beneath to clasp her around the waist, capture her bottom and lift her against the heavy ridge in his jeans.

He tore his mouth away first. 'How do you feel about being a little late for our presser?' he said, nuzzling her neck in the spot he'd found last night that he knew would drive her wild.

She pushed the fear aside to concentrate on the now.

'We can't be late, but we could be quick,' she gasped, her hands gripping his T-shirt and pulling it out of his jeans, the knowledge that he was all hers, at least for a little while, so intoxicating it hurt.

CHAPTER FOURTEEN

'HOW ARE YOU, Jamilla? In the pictures I saw of the Serrano Academy visit yesterday you looked radiant. But I just wanted to check in with you.'

'Honestly, I'm good, Orla,' Jamilla said, aware of her skin flushing. Thank goodness the Queen hadn't called her on a video app. 'Just a minute,' she said before covering the mouthpiece.

She hurried across the sitting room to the suite's bedroom door. Could Orla hear Dane taking a shower in the en suite bathroom? The thought only mortified her more. She closed the door carefully, aware of the strange feeling of unreality.

Orla was a friend, a good friend, and she'd been nothing but supportive, but Jamilla still wasn't used to being the focus of so much media attention. And she was becoming more and more concerned about the endless speculation in the media about her and Dane's relationship—it refused to die, and had only become more intense since they'd arrived in Spain for the last leg of the tour—despite her endless denials.

What was even more concerning, though, was how the media attention was starting to mess up her own perceptions.

She had seen the pictures taken yesterday too, had cringed at the string of increasingly lurid headlines.

The Prince and the Political Aide
Love on Tour?
How a Billionaire Nightclub Magnate was
Seduced into Becoming a Prince!

The articles accompanying those headlines had been equally ludicrous—full of barely concealed innuendo about her role in Dane's supposed transformation. But it was the photograph which Orla had just described which had stopped her breath ten minutes ago, when she'd been checking the media coverage of yesterday's assignments while waiting for Dane to appear.

The photographer had captured her and Dane in a rare and revealing private moment during yesterday's tour of a girls' school in Barcelona. She could still see the secretive little smile on her lips, the vivid blush on her cheeks and the incandescent light in her eyes as Dane leant close to her while a line of teenage girls stood behind them both.

She could still remember exactly what he'd whispered to her in that moment, his voice wry and wicked, to make the spontaneous smile appear.

'I always thought good girls were overrated. Who knew?'

She had been expecting Orla's call ever since the ball in Paris, when the press furore over the showdown between her father and Dane had hit the headlines.

Dane had fielded all the questions that day— refusing point-blank to answer any personal questions, but it hadn't deterred the media in the least.

He'd been calm, confident, supremely arrogant, every inch a prince. And she'd sat there like a dummy, tongue-tied and embarrassed, but also pathetically grateful for his sturdy presence as the questions were fired at them like missiles.

Her father had, of course, given an exclusive interview about her failings as a daughter to a highbrow French publication the next day— which had immediately been recycled and extensively quoted in every gossip rag, celebrity blog and tabloid magazine—only making the press attention worse once they'd arrived in Spain.

She hated that she had become the story in the past week. But what disturbed her more was how much she had come to rely on Dane's support, his protection. When they'd arrived at

Madrid-Barajas Airport and he'd shielded her from the waiting paparazzi to usher her safely into the limo. At the state banquet the following night, when he'd stayed by her side throughout. During the tour of a fruit market in Seville, when he'd included her in every photo op, much to the joy of the press. And of course at the girls' academy yesterday, the day after they'd arrived in Barcelona.

But much more disturbing than that was how she'd come to rely on him when they weren't under media scrutiny. In the evenings, when they sneaked back to his suite and he slammed the door shut, to take her in his arms and make fast, furious love to her. Or during those late-night meals, while she tried to discuss the itinerary for the next day and he distracted her all too easily, before devouring her all over again.

How had she come to revel in every touch—both tender and voracious? How had she found it so easy to let her mind drift on the tide of endorphins without having to engage with the truth…? How had she become so addicted to falling asleep in his arms, and waking up with him wrapped around her, usually hard and ready for more sleepy lovemaking before they showered and changed and sat down for breakfast to prepare for another day?

How had she been able to let herself forget—for six glorious days and nights—about the reckoning that awaited her when she returned to Zafar, and the tour—and this not-so-secret affair—was over?

'Are you sure, Jamilla?' She could hear Orla's concern from the other side of the continent. 'You looked so…' her friend's voice drifted into silence '…happy,' she managed at last.

'I'm so sorry, Orla. I feel as if I've let you and Karim down. That I've let Zafar down. The tour has become about whether or not we're in a relationship when it was never supposed to be.' The words came tumbling out as the shame Jamilla had been keeping so carefully at bay tightened her stomach into a knot.

She should never have agreed to stay with Dane after their night together in Paris. But, even before that, she'd lost perspective. She'd become entranced by him, ever since she'd seen the pain in his eyes when he'd spoken of his father, and she'd allowed her heart to believe there was a connection between them.

'Jamilla, what on earth are you talking about?' Orla interrupted her panicked confession. 'The tour has been a massive success. To be honest, your obvious…' she paused '…affection for one another has given the whole enterprise much more attention than we could ever have dreamt of. But, frankly, that's what concerns me. The intrusion has been immense, and I know you're not used to that sort of media focus.'

'Honestly, Orla, that's not a problem. And Dane has been wonderful,' Jamilla said quickly. Yes, she'd found the intrusion hard, because she simply wasn't used to the spotlight. But wasn't that the price she deserved to pay, for agreeing to spend her nights in Dane's suite? For leaping into this affair like a woman possessed. For allowing her pleasure to take precedent over her common sense, and her dedication to her job. They had been lucky that the publicity had actually worked in their favour. But it wasn't the thought of how unprofessional she'd allowed herself to become that terrified her now.

'I've noticed how attentive Dane has been too,' Orla said. 'And that's really why I called to check on you,' her friend added.

Jamilla frowned, confused. Where was this leading?

'Jamilla, in the pictures I saw yesterday…' Orla paused again. 'You don't need to tell me if there is anything between you, but you look…' She sighed. 'You look like a woman who has fallen in love.'

The words dropped into Jamilla's consciousness like a stone. And all the things she had avoided admitting, avoided even thinking about in the last week, perhaps even longer than that, coalesced in her stomach like an unexploded bomb. All the things she had come to rely on, to relish, to revel in.

Not just Dane's touch, but those long looks at her over the breakfast table. Those wry smiles of approval whenever they were working together. The attentive way he listened to her, as if everything she said mattered. The quiet times at night, after they had made love, when he held her close and she heard his heart slow. Even the moments when they argued about the itinerary—him trying to shorten every assignment so they could return to the suite sooner rather than later. The memory of their first kiss, as the Roman dawn spread across the horizon. Their wild ride on the bike. The sight of him charging across the ballroom to lift her father to his toes. The fierce compassion in his voice when he'd told her she deserved better than François Xavier Roussel.

Even that silly comment about good girls, designed to make her laugh, which had also lifted her heart. And made it pound so hard against her ribcage she'd been unable to control the tell-tale smile which had spread across her cheeks and made her eyes shine.

What if this *was* more than just infatuation? An endorphin rush she couldn't control? What if it was far worse than that? What if Orla were right, and she had lost her heart to this forceful, fascinating and completely unavailable man?

'I… I don't think that's true.' She forced the denial out, desperately trying to believe it. 'It's just that Dane's quite overwhelming,' she said, then realised what she'd let slip.

It was official, she was actually losing her mind. She hadn't meant to tell Orla that.

'So you are sleeping together,' Orla said, with a gentle acceptance of Jamilla's subterfuge which only made her feel worse about the deception.

'Yes, but that's really all it is,' she said quickly, trying to convince herself as much as Orla. 'It's just... I've never had a lover before and...'

'Jamilla, I had no idea he was your first lover.' Concern thickened Orla's voice and Jamilla wished desperately she hadn't blurted out the truth, suddenly realising it only made her sound more vulnerable and immature. 'I love Dane like a brother,' Orla added. 'But he and Karim both had difficult childhoods and I'm not sure he's very reliable...'

'Honestly, Orla, it's not a big deal,' Jamilla asserted, interrupting her friend, the comment about Dane's childhood making her heart stutter at the thought of the young boy who had been neglected by both his parents.

At least she'd always had her mother. But she'd come to realise over the last few weeks— not just from what she'd found out about Dane's past but also from the way he seemed able to so easily separate his emotions from the intimacy they'd shared—that he had spent a lot of his life protecting himself from rejection. So much so that she already suspected he would never open himself to more.

How could she have forgotten that so easily, allowed herself to dream, the way her mother had? It was foolish—beyond foolish—it was positively self-destructive.

'All I'm trying to say is,' she continued, 'this affair is about sex and endorphins. And I'm totally good with that. I watched my mother spend her life invested in a love that wasn't real. I'd never be foolish enough to do the same. Even if I wanted to be with him long-term, which I don't, Dane isn't the man for me.' But even as she said it she could feel the panic wrapping around her heart like an anaconda.

Was she her mother's daughter after all? Needy, desperate, wanting more than she could ever have from a man who couldn't—or wouldn't—give it to her?

She ended the call with Orla, having reassured her friend and employer that her affair with Dane Jones was never meant to last. But as she switched off her phone and placed it on the table with trembling fingers she knew she would have a much bigger task convincing herself.

'Even if I wanted to be with him long-term, which I don't, Dane isn't the man for me.'

Listening to Jamilla's words as she spoke on

the phone reverberated in Dane's skull. He stood with his shoulder propped on the bedroom door frame and watched her place her phone back on the table.

He crossed his arms, tried to focus on all the things that he had been looking forward to while he'd dressed.

Today's helicopter ride to Lisbon with Jamilla running through the itinerary in the seat next to him while he tried to distract her. The evening banquet with a consortium of dull European business leaders, the tedious conversation enlivened by the game of footsie he had planned to play with her under the table.

And all the memories of the last week which had made him whistle in the shower for the first time in his life.

Jamilla coming apart in his arms last night, her throaty cries spurring him on as he worked the spot with ruthless efficiency he knew would make her climax. The feel of her arms—strong and tight—around him, the scent of her hair—spicy and sweet—as they'd drifted into sleep. The vicious moment of panic when he'd woken up alone this morning, the bed beside him empty, only to relax when he'd heard her on the phone in the sitting room. The decision in the shower to tempt her back into bed before they left for the day—so he could feed the hunger that would not die. Not just for her, but for that soft smile, that sweet shyness beneath the efficiency, the eloquent compassion he'd spotted so many times in the past week—hell, the past three weeks.

But even as he tried to regain that easy balance, that heady feeling of anticipation…the words he'd just overheard made his stomach burn, taking him back to the child he'd been in Zafar, being led to the waiting helicopter by his mother's assistant. Crying as his father turned away from him to return to the palace without a backward glance.

And, worse, that sickening day six years later when his mother had screamed at him—in a fit of temper—the real reason his father had never replied to any of his letters…

A moment he'd spent the rest of his life determined to ignore, determined never to care about…never to let it matter to him.

'Even if I wanted to be with him long-term, which I don't, Dane isn't the man for me.'

The pain clamped around his ribs like a vice, making his breathing laboured and his heart hurt. Why was that? Why should he care what Jamilla thought of him, that she could never love him, when he didn't love her? This connection had only ever been about sex; they'd agreed upon that, right from the start. She'd wanted to keep their liaison a secret and he'd never had a problem with that…had he?

But, even as he tried to convince himself, the vice around his ribs tightened. He straightened away from the door, cleared his throat.

Jamilla swung around, her eyes widening as she spotted him in the doorway. 'Hi, Dane. You're dressed,' she said, the tell-tale blush on her cheeks. But he could see something in her eyes. Had she realised he'd heard her? Had she meant for him to hear?

He'd always found the way she flushed so easily every time she laid eyes on him a major turn-on. Now was no exception as the inevitable heat pooled in his groin. But his instant, unstoppable reaction only made the twist and burn in his gut more vicious. He ground his teeth to stop the turmoil of emotions from showing on his face. Or pouring out of his mouth.

Because that would make him weak. Something he had never been. Not since he was a little boy, writing those damn letters and kidding himself that one day his father would write back.

He strode across the room and cradled her cheek, vindicated by the warmth of her blush and the awareness that darkened her eyes, her response instant and unequivocal.

This was about hunger, not need. What the hell was he getting so worked up about anyway?

She *was* his. All his. In the only way he wanted.

'That can easily be remedied,' he said, keeping the ruthless desire at bay.

You're not that dumb kid any more, needing validation, needing acceptance.

'We don't have time.' She drew back but, instead of letting his hand fall, he cupped her neck, tugged her back.

'Sure we do—we've got twenty minutes,' he said, the strange feeling of loss turning the pain in his chest to a hollow ache. He bent to fasten his lips on the flutter of her pulse, determined to make her ache too, as he flicked open the buttons on her blouse with ruthless purpose. 'More than enough time to get us both off.'

Her breath caught, probably at the crude statement, but her body reacted instinctively, leaning into his caresses as her nipples hardened beneath his questing fingers. He scooped the swollen flesh out of her bra. The musky scent of her arousal turned his erection to iron, but did nothing to soothe the aching pain in his gut. And before he could stop himself the need he didn't want to feel, didn't even want to acknowledge, consumed him.

'Do you want me, Jamilla?' he asked, but he could already see she did, her passion at fever-pitch.

Snapping the hook on her bra, he captured one stiff peak with his mouth, then the other, suckled hard as she shuddered with reaction.

The need became frantic, desperate, clawing at his self-control and exposing that lonely, vulnerable part of himself he thought he'd destroyed long ago.

Just once more.

If he could have her just one more time it would be enough. That was all he wanted now. All he had ever wanted.

He pulled her round, bent her over the sitting room chair. Her breath came out in ragged pants as he lifted the pencil skirt, released the painful erection from his pants.

He didn't want to see her face, didn't want to drown in that look that had fooled him…and made him want more. When he could never have more. Should never need more.

His fingers found the slick bud of her clitoris. She jerked, wet and ready for him. He found the condom in his pocket, somehow managed to roll it on despite the frenzy churning inside him as he stroked her with ruthless determination.

At last, he edged the gusset of her panties to one side and placed the thick head of his erection at the tight entrance.

'Tell me again you want me,' he demanded as he held her breasts, poised to take her. Wild now, to control the pain that threatened to consume him. A pain he couldn't—wouldn't—acknowledge.

'I… I want you,' she groaned, sounding shocked, wary, confused, but as desperate as he.

He sank inside her in one brutal thrust, fill-ing her to the hilt, feeling her stretch to accommodate him. She was already coming, the soft cries, the tight heat driving him mad—with lust and grief—as he began to move.

You're mine. You're mine. You're mine, his mind shouted as he rocked hard and deep, giving her all of himself. But even as the ruthless climax clawed at his self-control, promising untold pleasure, the pain of her rejection bit into his heart.

She didn't want him. However much he might want her.

As the orgasm slammed into him at last, he emptied himself into the void. And the hopes and dreams he hadn't even admitted existed died, leaving only the great gaping hole of loneliness behind.

CHAPTER FIFTEEN

JAMILLA SHUDDERED. DANE'S penis was still huge inside her. Her heart thundered so hard she could almost feel it shattering.

His fingers dug into her hips. 'Don't move,' he grunted.

She held still, struggling to get her breath back, aware of the tenderness in her body, and the elemental sadness in her heart.

Why had that felt like more than sex…so much more? When she knew it wasn't.

He softened at last, then pulled out of her. She gasped, her swollen flesh releasing him with difficulty.

She struggled to pull down her skirt, brutally aware of how she must look. Standing upright, she hooked her bra, began to frantically redo her buttons, the sting of tears threatening to well over her lids as she saw one button had been torn off in his frenzy to have her.

She felt as if she had survived a hurricane. Or had she? Because the shimmer of afterglow from the brutally intense orgasm was doing nothing to control the longing shattering her heart.

She wanted this to mean more than it did.

She gulped down the sob working its way up her throat and continued to button her blouse right up to the neck. 'I should have a shower,' she said, suddenly desperate to escape from him and the panicked direction of her own thoughts.

But as she turned to leave he grasped her wrist. 'Look at me,' he demanded.

Her gaze rose to his, scared she would see contempt, judgement. Or, worse, indifference.

But what she saw made the agony back up in her throat and swell to impossible proportions. Not contempt, not judgement but regret.

Why did that only make the sadness swell, the tears threaten to overflow?

'I'm sorry,' he said, and the lump in her throat threatened to choke her.

What was he apologising for? Could he see the yearning in her heart? Did he know she'd lost all perspective?

'What...what for?' she asked.

He continued to watch her, and she suspected he could see right through her desperate ploy to appear unmoved, unshattered, undevastated.

'When we get to Lisbon I won't come to your suite again,' was all he said, with a finality that pierced her heart.

She wanted to argue with him, to tell him how she felt about him. To tell him she loved him.

But what would be the point? This affair had only ever been about one thing for him. And now, after that last cataclysmic joining, he'd finished with her.

It hurt, but only because she'd allowed herself to become delusional.

So she nodded. 'Okay,' she said, then turned and walked into the bedroom they'd shared the night before, holding her head high and refusing to look back.

Even once.

Until she'd walked into the bathroom, locked the door, and her legs gave way beneath her.

She discovered later that afternoon that she wasn't pregnant. She should have been relieved, but somehow the empty space in her womb felt like another cruel trick.

She whispered the news to him on the Zafari royal jet en route to Portugal. The sadness engulfed her again when he showed no reaction, not even relief. He simply stared back at her then nodded.

Two days later, the morning after their final assignment in Lisbon—during which she had been far too aware of him keeping his distance—she arrived at his suite to bid him goodbye, only to discover he had caught an earlier flight home to Manhattan.

By the time she arrived back in Zafar the next day, the speculation about their grand love affair had become little more than a footnote in the press. But the gaping hole remained in her heart.

The good girl was gone for ever, but the woman who had replaced her was little more than a shadow. She needed to know, she decided, why he had cut her off so easily and so comprehensively. Why had she been so wrong about where they might be heading? Was this really about her, or about something that had happened before she'd ever known him, before she'd loved him?

It took her most of the day to pack up her belongings. Then she emailed her resignation to Orla and Karim.

Before waiting for a reply, she left the Palace of the Kings for the last time on her mare Sana, with a pack of supplies and a bundle of old letters in her saddlebags.

Letters she hoped would give her some insight into the mind of a man who had been tender and passionate and possessive, but determined never to need her, the way she had come to need him.

CHAPTER SIXTEEN

Why aren't you answering your phone? We need to talk.

DANE STARED AT the latest message from Karim, but as his thumb hovered over the delete button the ringtone sounded, startling his horse, Tucker.

'Hey, boy, cool it,' he said, calming the thoroughbred Kentucky quarter horse. Jumping down, he threw the reins over the corral fence, then stared at his phone some more, which was still playing the theme tune from *Game of Thrones,* which he used for Karim.

Talk to him, get it over with, then move on.

It had been over a week since he'd sneaked out of Lisbon on an early-morning flight. Over a week since he'd taken Jamilla as if he owned her, pounding into her, trying to brand her as his when she'd already rejected him. Over a week since his life had disintegrated. He couldn't sleep, couldn't eat and couldn't stop thinking about her.

He dreamt about her constantly. Imagined those moments: when she'd looked at him out of the corner of her eye, excitement and compassion making the amber sparkle; when he'd woken up with her soft butt pressed against his arousal, her spicy sultry scent surrounding him; when she'd cajoled, directed and nudged him into becoming a halfway decent prince; when she'd spoken about her jerk of a father with that lost look in her eyes; when she'd danced the night away in his arms and made him see for the first time who she really was—a fiercely passionate, genuine, incredibly beautiful woman who could never be his.

Patting Tucker's rump, he walked round the horse, leapt over the corral fence, then clicked the phone's answer button before he could second-guess himself again.

Karim would have news of Jamilla. And he wanted to know how she was doing.

'Hey, bro,' he said, the relaxed tone not even convincing him. 'What's up?'

'Dane, where are you? I've been trying to contact you for nearly a week.' His brother's voice sounded strained.

'At the farm,' he said. 'What's wrong—is something up with Orla? Or Hasan?' he asked, suddenly realising his brother's desire to contact him might not actually be about him. Or Jamilla.

Or the way he'd managed to screw up the one favour his brother had asked him in thirty years.

'Orla's good. Although she's not enjoying this pregnancy. At least the morning sickness has calmed down a bit and the doctors are not as worried about the hypertension at the moment. Hasan's good too, into everything and driving all three of us nuts,' his brother said, his voice softening in the way it always did when he referred to his wife and child.

'Okay, good to know,' Dane replied, not surprised by the swift spike of jealousy. His chest tightened, the emptiness still there from a week ago, when Jamilla had told him she'd had her period. Dumb, really, because an unplanned pregnancy would have been a disaster. Wouldn't it? He had lost her before he'd ever had her. And he knew why, because he was and always had been damaged goods. His old man had figured it out by the time he was five. 'So why so desperate to talk to me?' Dane asked, trying to stop his mind going over those unpleasant thoughts all over again.

Karim and he were close enough, but it wasn't as if they spoke to each other constantly.

He heard Karim's sigh. 'Mostly, I just wanted to thank you properly, for doing the tour. I know it was way outside your comfort zone and I wanted you to know how much Orla and I appreciated you stepping in like that. And how impressed I was that you made such a success of it.'

'Are you serious?' Was his brother making fun of him? Because it was the last thing he needed. The whole experience had already messed with his head and his equilibrium. He didn't even know any more who he was, or who he wanted to be. All he knew was that he wasn't enough.

'Absolutely,' Karim replied, sounding genuine. 'Why wouldn't I be?'

'Because we both know I messed it up,' he shot back. The horse whinnied behind him and he lowered his voice and stepped away from the corral. The late summer sunshine warmed his skin, but the cold weight in his belly refused to budge. The weight that had been there ever since he'd walked out of the hotel, knowing that the woman in front of him was everything he wanted but couldn't have.

He'd been there before, as a boy. When he'd acted out so his mother would notice him—she hadn't—or sent increasingly desperate letters to his father, telling him the truth about his home life so he might step in and take him back to Zafar—and his father hadn't even bothered to open the damn letters.

He hated that kid.

'I jumped her when I had no right to touch her. Luckily for both of us, she figured it out though.'

The words tumbled out, his voice breaking on the wave of misery he'd kept so carefully at bay for over a week.

'*Whoa*, Dane, take it easy.' His brother's deep calming voice reminded him of their boyhood, when he had always been there to soothe the futile tears. 'Are you talking about Jamilla?'

'Yeah,' he said, humiliation joining the other emotions making the lead weight plunge. 'How is she?' he asked, because there wasn't much point in keeping the desire to know more about her a secret any longer. He'd already spilled his guts. 'Have you spoken to her since the tour ended?'

'No.' He could hear his brother swallowing. 'She resigned.'

'She…she what?' Why would she do that? Sick dread joined the misery. Had he done this too—ruined her career somehow?

'She quit,' Karim reiterated. 'And then disappeared. Orla hasn't been able to reach her in Zafar. Even Saed—our all-seeing household manager—has no idea where she went. We figured her disappearance probably had something to do with you—which was kind of the other reason I wanted to speak to you.' His brother paused, and Dane could hear the hesitation. But instead of sounding furious when he continued, all Karim sounded was concerned. 'What exactly happened between you two? Because you looked really good together in all the press photographs. When you were here in Kildare, seeing you with her… I thought maybe…maybe there was more there for you than just a convenient hook-up.'

There was no judgement in the observation. But somehow that made it worse.

He deserved judgement. Hell, he deserved a damn good horse-whipping. The kind of whipping his father had given Karim more than once. But had never given him.

He thrust his fingers through his hair. Damn, exactly how screwed-up was he that he'd rather get whipped than be ignored? Or rejected.

'It *was* more…' he said, blurting out the truth.

'Then why did you break up with her? And why did you keep the affair a secret?' His brother's pragmatic questions reverberated in his chest.

Because she didn't want me.

But the answer that he had told himself for more than a week—the answer that had given him a convenient get-out clause when he'd needed it—didn't seem so damn convenient any more. Because he could finally see it for what it was. An excuse, an easy out, a way of never facing the demons that had chased him for most of his life.

He wanted more from Jamilla than sex. He had done almost as soon as he'd touched her.

Heck, the minute he'd laid eyes on her and seen the sharp intelligence and feisty spirit behind the mask of perfection. But he had been more than happy to accept those parameters, because he'd been too scared to ask for more. In case she rejected him. And when he'd heard what she'd said to Orla, he'd taken it at face value. He hadn't confronted her, hadn't told her how he felt. Because he hadn't wanted to risk the fallout if he laid his heart on the line and she kicked it to the kerb. He hadn't been straight with her. Hell, he hadn't even been straight with himself. And finally he knew the real answer to Karim's question.

'Because I'm a coward,' he said.

His brother let out a heavy sigh. 'You're not a coward, Dane. But it's not me you've got to convince. It's yourself. And Jamilla. If you want her back, that is?'

Yes, I do.

Karim's quietly spoken question had the dam breaking inside him, the need flooding through.

His brother was right. What was he doing hiding out and licking his wounds in upstate New York when he should be in Zafar, tracking down the woman he'd thrown away so carelessly?

If he put himself out there and she told him he wasn't enough it would hurt like hell, but what would hurt more was never knowing what they might have had.

Because he'd been too much of a coward to even ask.

CHAPTER SEVENTEEN

Dear Father

Mom wants me to ask you for money again. But I don't have to, because she never reads the letters I send you. I know you're mad at her. I'm mad at her too. We moved again last month. I put the new address on this envelope—so if you want to send me a letter you can. I've also got an email address, if you want to talk that way.

Could I come over to Zafar this summer? While Karim is there? I won't get in the way, I swear. You won't even probably know I'm there. I don't cry all the time like I used to. Perhaps I could help out in the stables. I love horses, even though we live in the city. And I haven't forgotten how to ride.

Do you still have the black Arabian with the white socks? I rode him a couple of times with Karim and I didn't fall off.

Please write back, Father.

I won't tell Mom you did.
Your son,
Dane

JAMILLA FOLDED THE old letter and sniffed loudly.

Reading Dane's letters to his father had been a mistake. Because she could feel the desperation of the boy in every word, the need to connect with a man who didn't want him.

It hurt to know that while she'd always had her mother—however broken, however sad—Dane had had no parent who cared for him.

Her head lifted at the sound of hoof beats from beyond the Bedouin tent. She reached for the pistol in her pack. Bandits were very rare in Zafar these days, but she was a woman alone in the desert and she wasn't taking any chances.

Wrapping her headscarf across her nose and mouth, she lifted the tent flap.

A rider approached over the dunes, on a black horse.

Reaction shimmered through her, followed by a twist of anxiety and panic, and the heavy weight of grief.

Dane?

What was he doing here? Had he come to reject her again? And how had he found her? Only her mother's family knew this spot, a place she had come often when she was a teenager, not long after her mother's death.

He pulled the powerful stallion to a stop in front of her, then jumped down in one fluid movement.

'Jamilla,' he said as he draped the horse's reins over the corral fence and strode towards her. 'What the hell are you doing out here alone?'

She lifted the pistol. 'I am well protected,' she said, even as she could feel her heart shattering all over again. She shouldn't have read his letters, because she could see the little boy who hid inside the man. The child she had come to know in the last few days, as she'd read about the neglect in his own words.

But this wasn't the boy; it was the man. The man who didn't want her. Couldn't love her. Would never want more from her than sex.

'How did you find me?' she asked.

And why?

Why had he come to Zafar? Why had he followed her here when he had discarded her so easily a week ago?

'Your mother's father was surprisingly cooperative when I spoke to him on the phone and he figured out who I was. Apparently the speculation about our secret romance reached the Zafari press too.'

So it was still a joke to him.

A fortifying anger stirred the anguish, making her stomach feel like a black hole—an anger she clung to now. 'Please leave. I do not want you here, nor do I need your protection.'

But as she turned to return into the tent he grasped her arm and tugged her back round to face him. 'Why did you resign?'

That piercing blue gaze, the gaze she saw in her sleep now, searched her face with an intensity that made her skin flare with sensation and her heart pummel her ribcage.

She yanked her arm out of his grasp, suddenly furious—with herself as much as him. How could she still respond so easily, yearn for him so much—a man who had made it very clear he felt nothing for her?

'Not that it's any of your business, but I resigned because I needed a new challenge. Somewhere far from Zafar.' Where she would not be constantly dogged by the reminders of how she'd failed herself.

And even if the ambition to see and experience more in her life felt hollow now, and empty, it didn't mean she couldn't nurture it. She refused to be that sheltered woman who had concentrated on her career—and had fallen too easily for a pipedream.

The frown on his forehead and the doubtful expression in his eyes made it clear he didn't believe her. 'You're sure about that?' he asked. 'You're sure you're not just running again? From me?'

The accusation felt like a dart to her heart.

'I wasn't the one who ran,' she said, suddenly tired of the lies and evasions. 'I read the letters, the ones you wrote to your father,' she said, and saw him flinch. 'So I know you lied about them. You were a little boy who needed someone to show him he was valued, he mattered. I know what that feels like. I would have understood, if you'd trusted me.'

He stiffened, the guarded look, the wary tension in his body rejecting the truth even now. She wasn't having it, not any more. Hadn't they both run from the truth—that the rejections they'd suffered in childhood had made them both cowards? But she was through being a coward. He'd come all this way; he deserved to know how she really felt. No more evasions.

'I was falling in love with you. You made me feel valued, important, cherished. But you threw me away,' she finished, glad when she managed to keep her voice firm, level, despite the agony twisting her guts.

She blinked, letting the tear fall. She brushed it away with her fist. She'd given him all the power in their relationship, let him set all the terms. So who was really to blame for this crippling heartache?

'You need to go now.'

'Wait… No.' The words exploded out of Dane's chest.

He'd travelled through the night to get to

Zafar, a place he'd always hated, tracked down Jamilla's family, had to phone her very disapproving grandfather. And then he'd taken his brother's stallion Azzam out before dawn to ride here.

When he'd seen her, standing proud and alone in the entrance of the Bedouin tent she'd seemed like a goddess to him. And he'd known he would do anything to undo the wrongs he'd done her. But the fear and panic which had assailed him ever since he'd finally acknowledged the truth had refused to abate. And he'd screwed up all over again.

I was falling in love with you.

Was.

He caught up with her again, gripped her upper arm, felt the muscles tense. But the zing of attraction was nowhere near as terrifying as the driving need.

'You said you didn't want me, didn't want anything long-term. On the phone that day. To Orla. I heard you…' The accusation burst out, but even he could hear how lame it sounded.

He'd known, from the way she looked at him, touched him, supported him, they could have had so much more.

'I didn't… I didn't know you heard me say that.' Her eyes darkened with a sadness that made his ribs contract. 'I was scared. My feelings were so strong and Orla said… She said she thought I was falling in love. She was right, of course. But why didn't you tell me what you'd overheard?'

He shook his head. 'I should have, but that would mean admitting how I felt. I guess.'

Her brows rose and understanding crossed her face. An understanding he was sure he didn't deserve. 'Is that why you took me with such…desperation? Before you broke things off with me?'

'No… Yes…' He swore and let go of her arm, then thrust his fingers through his sweaty hair. He had to make this right. But how? 'Everything got so mixed up in my head. I lost my mind for a moment. I wanted more but I was too scared to admit it. Even to myself. And hearing you say that to Orla…it made me feel like that damn kid again. Always on the outside looking in.'

He looked away, unable to meet her eyes while he said what he had to say. She deserved to hear the truth. 'I want to be the guy you see when you look at me. But there's stuff you need to know.' He heaved a sigh. Stared out at the blue of the oasis near the tent, reminding him of another time, the day she had found him at the Halu Oasis, and everything had seemed so simple. 'You're so smart. And I didn't even graduate high school,' he began, determined to tell her everything. Every damn inadequacy that had haunted him for so long.

'Dane, that's ridiculous. You've built a multimillion-dollar business from nothing.' He heard the incredulous tone and almost laughed. 'The fact you didn't graduate only makes that achievement more impressive.'

He turned back, making himself meet her gaze. The laugh got stuck in his throat because he knew the biggest hurdle was yet to come.

Absorbing the sheen of moisture still lingering in her eyes, he murmured, 'I might not be his.'

Her brow furrowed. 'I'm sorry?'

'I might not be of royal blood,' he said again. 'She told me once, when she was hammered and strung out—she'd taken lovers. Because he had, and she wanted to spite him. The timing meant Abdullah may have been my father. But she couldn't be sure.' The crippling inadequacy threatened to choke him, but he forced himself to continue. 'I was eleven, maybe twelve. I stopped writing the letters after that. And she couldn't make me. I'd invested this whole identity in being his son, in being Karim's brother. I locked it all away, convinced myself it didn't matter. But when I heard you say that to Orla... I don't know, it made sense. Why would you want me, when I'm more than likely not the guy you think I am?'

Jamilla pressed her fingers to her lips, holding back the sob queueing up in her throat. But the tears fell freely down her cheeks now. Because she could see the boy now, inside the man, a shining light shadowed by uncertainty, as clearly as the sunlight glimmering on the water. She'd hurt him with the lie she'd told Orla. A lie she'd told to protect herself. Perhaps it had been bad timing, a foolish misunderstanding, something she had never intended for him to overhear. But if she'd been honest with him sooner, and herself, and told him how she really felt, her lie would have had no power to hurt him.

Reaching out, she touched his cheek. The day-old stubble abraded her palm as his jaw tensed. 'Dane, you must know, it doesn't matter to me who your biological father is… Or isn't. It's you I love.'

He covered her hand, his eyes flaring with an intensity that stole her breath. Dragging her hand down, he pressed it to his chest, making her aware of the thumping beat of his heart. 'You love me? Still… Even after everything I've…'

'Yes, yes, yes.' She pulled her hand free, threw her arms around his neck to press her body against his and shower him with kisses. All the fear was gone in a heartbeat, to be replaced with that painful bubble of hope. 'You idiot,' she said, drawing back.

He wrapped his arms around her waist, lifted her off the ground and squeezed her so tightly she felt sure he would never let her go again. 'Thank God.'

He buried his head against her neck, kissed the sensitive skin beneath her chin, caressing the pulse point with his lips. But as he scooped her up, to march with her into the tent, she wriggled free.

'What's the deal?' he asked, looking wonderfully confused.

'Don't you have something you want to tell me first?' she asked, part sass, part determination. And part panic.

'Yeah, I guess I do.' Her confidence surged again when his lips curled, but then, to her astonishment, he dropped to one knee.

'Dane, what are you…'

'Shh…' he said, clasping her hands in his and staring up at her, the humour gone, to be replaced with a focus so intense it made her ribs ache.

Even if Dane Jones wasn't a Khan by blood, he was—and always had been—every inch a prince.

'I absolutely adore you, Jamilla Omar Roussel. Your smarts, your sass, your beauty and your far too well-developed sense of what's right and what's wrong. And for all the sexy times you're only ever gonna get to have with me.'

Her face burned and he laughed, before

standing up to tower over her and pull her into his arms.

'I'm head over heels for those blushes too,' he murmured, placing a kiss on her lips that managed to be both tender and tantalising in equal measure. And only made the blush more vivid. 'I want us to build a life together,' he continued. 'I want you to have my babies. But, more than that, I want to marry you, because I love you. So, so much.'

She sank into the kiss, as ravenous and joyous as him.

When they finally came up for air and he scooped her back up into his arms, she clung to his broad shoulders and pressed her face into his chest to stop her buoyant heart from bursting right out of her chest and flying off into the cosmos.

EPILOGUE

Four months later

'YOUR HIGHNESS, A package arrived this morning at the palace for you…but addressed to me. It had this letter inside.'

Dane glanced up from his desk to find Hakim—the young valet who always attended him when he and Jamilla returned to Zafar—standing in the doorway of his study holding a large envelope and a curious expression.

Dane's heart battered his ribcage, his breath becoming trapped in his lungs, but somehow he managed to close his laptop, get up from the desk and cross the room without losing his cool. 'Great, thanks, I've been expecting it,' he said, pasting an easy smile on his face and taking the envelope from Hakim.

The young man nodded, keeping the obvious questions he wanted to ask to himself. Then he excused himself to prepare Dane's outfit for tonight's official naming ceremony.

Dane had asked specifically that the Narabian clinic send a letter instead of an email, and that they post the results care of his valet, to his apartment in the palace in Zafar and not the brownstone he'd recently purchased in Manhattan—where he and Jamilla had been living for most of the last four months, ever since their whirlwind elopement.

It had made sense to get the results sent here, he told himself staunchly. They were due to be here for a week, finishing off their visit tonight attending the state ceremony to declare Karim and Orla's twin daughters—Rana and Amina—heirs to the Zafari throne. But as he held the heavy cream cardboard envelope in his hand he knew those weren't the real reasons for keeping the test on the downlow. Not even close.

He had made Karim swear not to mention the DNA test to anyone, when he'd asked him to provide a cheek swab four days ago to have couriered to the clinic. Karim had been unhappy about the secrecy, and mad as hell about the fact Dane was taking the test at all.

'You're my brother, Dane, no matter what some damn DNA sample says. You understand? If you think you're getting out of your royal duties now on a technicality—or shirking your responsibility to Hasan and the girls as their uncle—you can forget it.'

His heart thundered in his ears at the memory

of Kasim's furious expression when he'd made the request. And the deep well of love for his brother that had spilled over in that moment.

He slid his thumb across the address of the fancy clinic on the back and his breathing eased a little.

Yeah, Karim wasn't wrong. No matter what was in here, they would still be brothers. Funny to think he'd spent so much of his life scared of finding out the truth about his heritage because he was terrified he'd lose that connection, without ever realising that what he shared with his brother went a great deal deeper than blood.

But it wasn't Karim's reaction he was concerned about. Not really.

It was Jamilla's.

He swallowed down the thick tide of dread in his throat. A dread that had been building for days, ever since she'd snuggled into his arms in their palace chambers after a tiring first day in Zafar spent getting acquainted with their new nieces and whispered, 'You were so wonderful with the babies, Dane. I think you'll make an amazing father…' But then she'd stiffened slightly and her voice had taken on a strangely tentative quality when she finally added, 'Some day.'

It hadn't been a question. After all, they'd spoken about having children before, when he'd first proposed to her. And she'd seemed keen.

But her slight hesitation that night had bothered him ever since.

At first he'd convinced himself it was because she simply wasn't keen to start trying too soon. He got that; they deserved more quality time, just the two of them, before they settled into the rigours of parenthood. The twins were cute as hell but they were also a lot of work, and while Karim and Orla looked ecstatic with their new babies, and Hasan had turned into an endlessly fascinating toddler, his brother and sister-in-law also looked exhausted.

Then there was the problem of Jamilla's career—which she had only just started establishing in New York. He could understand why she'd be reluctant to start a family before she'd got the new diplomatic mission she was managing in Manhattan for the Zafar monarchy properly established. But then again—because it was being run by his super-smart and super-efficient wife—it was already a roaring success, organising a wealth of new educational and cultural exchanges and travel and tourism opportunities between their two nations.

Jamilla had never again mentioned what he'd told her in the desert that day, the stuff his mom had claimed about his parentage. She'd told him then that his biological inheritance didn't matter to her, and he'd believed her. Absolutely.

But that conversation a week ago had played

over and over again in his head. Not least because holding Karim's tiny daughters in his arms had made the yearning in his chest that much worse.

What if Jamilla was having second thoughts? What if it did matter to her, even if only a little, that they didn't know for sure who he really was? Wasn't he robbing her of the chance to know who she'd really married?

Eventually, the damn questions had bugged him so much he'd decided the only way to get past them was to finally confront the truth. It was better to know—for her sake as well as his. If they were going to have kids, she had a right to know if they were of royal blood. They both did.

He flipped the envelope over, reached for the letter opener on his desk. But he couldn't seem to make his fingers stop trembling long enough to slit the paper open. And the long-ago fear roared back to life, like a fire-breathing dragon sitting under his breastbone, ready to burn his sense of identity, his sense of belonging right down to the ground all over again.

What the hell will you do if you don't get the answer you want, and it does make a difference to her after all, you dummy? Because no way in hell are you letting her go.

'Dane, what on earth are you doing hiding in here? Hakim is waiting for you to get changed.'

Jamilla stood on the threshold of her husband's study, happy to have found him.

But the nerves that had been tying her stomach in knots for days cinched tight when his head lifted and she saw the haunted look in his eyes she remembered from the first time he had returned to the Palace of the Kings.

'What is it? What's wrong?' she said, rushing into the room.

She hadn't seen that look for months now, even though they'd returned to the palace several times since their marriage. But the thought was quickly followed by panic.

Oh, God, had Orla told him what Jamilla had confided in her that morning? Surely she wouldn't have, even though her friend had been fairly unsubtle about her thoughts on the subject when the palace doctor had confirmed the results of Jamilla's blood test.

'Jamilla, you are joking? Dane absolutely adores you; it's plain for everyone to see. And he's wonderful with the twins and Hasan. You have to tell him; I think he'll be overjoyed.'

'But I was going to tell him my suspicions a week ago and...when I mentioned him being a father, he went so still, I just... I couldn't. It's too soon, it's totally unplanned. I just need more time.'

The choking panic closed around her throat again, but then she noticed the envelope in his hands.

'Dane? What is that?'

'Busted.' He handed the large, official-looking envelope to her and she read the clinic address on the back. 'You want to open it for me?' he asked as she realised what the envelope contained. 'Find out if I'm really a Khan or not.'

She stared at his face, her heart breaking at the tense look, the desperate attempt to appear nonchalant. She knew how much this meant to him, even though it shouldn't.

To her he would never just be someone's son, someone's brother, a Prince of Zafar by blood, or by shared history, or both. To her he was all those things and so much more.

He was her husband, her lover, her soulmate, her best friend. The person who made her laugh, who made her happy, who frustrated and teased and challenged and provoked her. The man who could make her skin tingle and her heart race with a single look. The man who had finally shown her what unconditional love and approval felt like. And who, by doing so, had made her the best person she could be.

But, even knowing all that about Dane, she nodded. She couldn't tell him any of that; he had to believe it himself.

'Okay, I'll open it and, whatever is in it, we'll deal with it together,' she said. Maybe he needed to take this step, to finally release him from the fears of his past so he could become fully invested in his future. In their future.

His lips quirked and some of that haunted look faded. 'So fierce,' he murmured.

She nodded, tears stinging her eyes at the appreciation in his voice. 'But first I have something to tell you,' she added.

Something, she realised, she should have told him ten days ago, when her period had failed to appear. And a week ago, when she'd had that first positive home pregnancy test, before she'd chickened out. Apparently her husband wasn't the only one still pandering to the insecurities of the past.

But that ended now.

She placed the envelope on his desk, then reached up to press her palms to the tight muscles in his jaw. 'I had it confirmed by the Palace doctor this morning... I'm pregnant.'

His brows shot up his forehead, those pure blue eyes widening. 'You're *what*?' his voice croaked out, his hands grasping her waist, holding on to her, the joy in his eyes banishing the last of that haunted look. For ever, she hoped.

She grinned. 'We're expecting a baby.' Her heart leapt into her throat at his stunned but ecstatic laugh.

It wasn't too soon. It could never be too soon. They were going to be parents, together. They both wanted this so much, and they would be good at it, so good, because they both knew far too much about how to be a bad parent.

'Oh. My. God.' His gaze dropped to her belly then shot back to her face. 'For real? *Already*?'

'Yes, for real. I'm not sure how it happened but...'

'Who cares?' he interrupted her. 'This is the best news ever.' Lifting her up, he spun her around. And when he finally dropped her back on her feet they were kissing, touching, loving each other, and she had totally resigned herself to being really late for the naming ceremony.

When they finally arrived in the palace court-yard—half an hour later—Jamilla was flushed and exhilarated and ready to face her future with courage and determination. While Dane stood beside her in his dress uniform, looking smugger than ever as they gave Karim and Orla their two pieces of exciting news.

In approximately seven and a half months' time she and Dane would be welcoming yet another brand-new member of the Zafar royal family—or, given the Khans' propensity for having twins, possibly two new members of the royal family.

And Dane was going to find it next to impossible to weasel out of his duties as a Prince of Zafar from then on because there was a ninety-nine point eight per cent probability that he was the current King's biological half-brother.

But in the end all four of them agreed only the

first bit of news really mattered—because there was no way in hell Karim and Orla would have let Dane off his royal duties ever again now, whatever the result of his DNA test.

* * * * *

If you were head over heels for
Banished Prince to Desert Boss
you're sure to love these other stories
by Heidi Rice!

The Royal Pregnancy Test
Innocent's Desert Wedding Contract
One Wild Night with Her Enemy
The Billionaire's Proposition in Paris
The CEO's Impossible Heir

Available now!